Moira Anne Brewer, was born in London, spent her teenage years in Dorset and has lived in Devon for over twenty years, the last eight of those in Torrington. She has worked as a bilingual secretary and as a teacher of French. She has always been a keen observer of people as well as being interested in the character and history of her local environment. Reflecting upon what life must have been like in Torrington in the past, particularly during the turbulent years of the Civil War, Moira embarked upon research of the period. A growing fascination with the subject led to the writing of this book. As well as writing, her pleasures include travel, singing, reading and spending time with her family.

Torrington Burning

Moira Brewer

Moira Brewer

CREEDY PUBLISHING
DEVON

CREEDY PUBLISHING
Creedy House
Warren Lane
Torrington
Devon
EX38 8DP

ISBN 0- 9528446- 0 -5

© Moira Brewer
   First published 1996

Torrington
Burning

This book is a work of fiction. The events and characters described in it are imaginary – with the exception of historic incidents and persons of note referred to by their true names. None of the imaginary characters are intended to represent specific living persons.

This book is sold subject to the condition that it shall not, by way of trade or otherwise, be lent, re-sold, hired out or otherwise circulated without the publisher's prior consent being given in writing, in any form of binding or cover other than that in which it is published and without a similar condition being imposed on the subsequent purchaser.

Typeset, Printed, and Bound by
The Lazarus Press
6 Grenville Street • Bideford
Devon • England • EX39 2EA

Cover Design by Peter Hayes, Photograph by Denis Tracey

In Memory of my father
Robert Alexander Pearce
an admirer of Cromwell

Acknowledgements

I should like to thank my husband, Bob, for his encouragement and support, Alison Harding for giving me the confidence to keep writing, and John Wardman for his interest and the loan of reference books.

My thanks also go to Tic Moore for her help with photocopying, to Bill O'Donnell, Roy Lee and Elizabeth Bowden for specialist information on historical details, varieties of wood and musical instruments respectively, and to John Broomhead and Andrew Tregoning for their time in helping to plan a cover design. For my eventual choice of cover, I thank Peter Hayes for his design and Denis Tracey for allowing me the use of his photograph.

I should like to thank Felicity Jones for typing my manuscript onto disk and Edward Gaskell of The Lazarus Press, Bideford, for making a professional job of producing this book.

Finally, I wish to thank David Nainby of Great Torrington School, The Mole and The Haggis Bookshop, M & V Ferry Hardware, Kimbers Antiques, and Youngs Newsagents for their help in publicising and selling my book.

M A B

ONE

If she climbed onto the gate, gathering up her skirts in one hand and clutching the gate post with the other, Faith could just see the sea. She gazed through the trees and across the rolling North Devon hills at this glimpse of the North Ocean as a shipwrecked man would stare yearningly at a distant vessel. Some days it shone silver in the sun, other days it was hazy and indistinct and she would imagine rather than see it.

'If 'ee can see the sea, 'tis about to rain; if 'ee can't see it, it be rainin' already!' old Joseph would say. Today was crisp and bright and full of promise and the sea glistened on the far horizon like the polished blade of a sword.

Faith had never been to the sea, having neither the opportunity nor the means to get there. The part of the coast nearest to her home was some ten miles distant and she dearly hoped to go there one day to see and hear the waves break on the shore, to breathe the salt air and to look out over the ocean and imagine what lands lay beyond.

'You still daydreamin', maid? Get they eggs in here right away!' Cook's raucous bark startled Faith out of her musing and she climbed down from the gate, took up the basket of eggs she had collected from the hen coop, and picked her way across the cobbled yard to the pantry door at the side of her master's house.

In the kitchen Joan Hutchings, known simply as 'Cook' by everyone in the household, was baking at the scrubbed wooden table which filled the centre of the room. She stood with feet planted solidly apart, sleeves rolled up to her elbows and plump forearms covered in flour.

'I want them eggs over here,' she demanded. 'I need four for me cake, d'reckly. You can start beatin' them in that bowl ready for me when I've finished this pie crust.'

'Yes, certainly, Cook,' Faith said in her most sweetly obedient manner.

'And none of your lip!' Cook scowled, thumping a huge lump of dough onto the floured table top. She blinked in the rising white haze of flour and waved her heavy wooden rolling pin in Faith's direction.

Faith cracked four eggs into the bowl Cook had pushed towards her and beat them vigorously with a fork in time to a song she hummed to herself:

'Now is the month of Maying,
When merry lads are playing,
Fa la la la la la la la la,
Fa la whisk whisk whisk whisk WHISK!'

Just then the door from the passageway opened a crack and a little blond head peeked around.

'Hello there, my beauty! Come to see Cookie?'

It was like the sun coming out on a cloudy day with Cook when that child appeared. Eleanor, at six, was the youngest of the de Bere family. Unlike her brothers and sister, she did not consider it beneath her to come into the kitchen. The soft leather soles of her little slippers pattered on the stone floor as she trotted across the room to Cook and raised her arms so that she could be lifted up onto a stool at Cook's side.

Cook tied a protective teacloth round the little girl's waist and gave her a small lump of pastry dough. 'You can make me some jam tarts, my lover,' she coaxed the child, fetching a small-sized rolling pin and a round metal pastry cutter from a drawer in the table. Eleanor was in her element clutching, flattening and cutting her pastry. Looking up at Cook, a smudge of flour on her button nose and another lodged in her eyebrow where she had rubbed her eye, she said: 'Did you know, Cookie, my papa and my brother, Wreford, are with the Queen?'

Wreford! Merely the mention of her young master's name caused Faith to shiver and to falter momentarily in her egg-beating.

'Are they now? And where be that?' Cook looked down fondly at Eleanor who was gazing at her so earnestly as she squeezed the sticky remains of her pastry between dainty childish fingers.

'They are taking her to Cornwall and then she's going to France. It's her home. She's French, you know.' The wide blue eyes moved from Cook to Faith to include her in this important piece of information.

'Why is Queen Henrietta Maria going off to France just now?' Faith asked the child and was treated to a dark warning glance from Cook. Little Eleanor was undismayed and addressed Faith as a patient schoolmaster might instruct his ignorant pupil.

'There are evil men about who wish to harm the King and Queen and they are coming this way. The Queen is weak and ill after having her baby and so the King wishes her to be safe, away from danger.'

'And has she taken her baby with her?' Faith

persisted, unable to imagine leaving her baby for other people to look after and interested to hear what the child had been told. But Cook intervened.

'Of course not! A queen doesn't look after her own baby, there's a wet nurse for that. The young Princess will be quite safe in Exeter. Now, how're these tarts coming along? Let's find the blackcurrant jelly.' And Cook lifted Eleanor off her stool so they could go to the pantry together and look amongst the jars of fruit conserve lined up on the shelves.

As they returned with a pot of jelly, there was a stamping of heavy work-boots outside the door into the yard and old Joseph came in through the pantry, staggering slightly under the weight of a basket full of logs which he set down with a thump by the fire.

'There 'ee are, Cook. That'll get the fire nice 'n hot for your cooking. What's to eat, today?' He lowered himself, old bones creaking, onto a stool by the hearth and, reaching into a pocket of his jerkin, pulled out a clay pipe which he proceeded to stuff with coarse tobacco from an old leather pouch he had found in another pocket.

Cook looked at him with ill-concealed irritation as he stuck his pipe between his remaining teeth, lit the tobacco with a taper from the fire and puffed clouds of foul-smelling smoke up towards the ceiling.

'Herring pie, already in the oven, but there's a while till dinner time. Can't you find something to do, or are you gonna be sittin' there under my feet?'

'Reckon so,' grunted Joseph and gave Faith a sidelong wink.

Cook considered the kitchen to be her domain and got annoyed with anyone cluttering it up, especially if they were sitting around, relaxing. Joseph, however, was unmoved. He had been with the family since General de Bere was a lad, mainly as the groom until he became too old to handle the horses. Then Faith's brother, Amos, had been taken on and Joseph taught him all he knew. The de Beres had kept him on as a reward for all his years of loyal service and he did odd jobs about the house and estate. He felt thoroughly at home and was not intimidated by Cook's sharp comments.

'Any chance of a pot of ale for an old fella who's been choppin' wood?' he wheedled, his dark eyes still sharp in his lined, weather-beaten face.

'Can't you see when a body's busy?' snapped Cook. 'I must get this little lady's hands clean before returning her to her mama.'

'I'll get it,' Faith offered, putting down the bowl of butter and sugar she had been creaming while Cook helped Eleanor put a blob of jam on each of her pastry circles and stowed them for her into the oven by the hearth along with the herring pie. Faith picked up the leather-jack from the table and filled it from the barrel out in the pantry and fetched a tankard, setting them side-by-side on the edge of the hearth next to Joseph. Cook had taken Eleanor out into the yard to wash her hands under the pump.

'Cook's as soft as butter with that child,' Faith remarked, taking up the bowl once again and beating eggs and sifting flour into the cake mixture and stirring with a wooden spoon.

"Tis probably 'cos she lost her own maid when her was a little 'un,' Joseph said, matter-of-factly, pouring ale from the leather-jack into his tankard with a less than steady hand.

'I didn't think she had any children.'

'Her was the only one.'

'How did she die?' Faith stopped stirring and stared at the old man perched on his stool with his wrinkled woollen stockings and his breeches, baggy around his shrivelled shanks, and his sparse grey hair falling to the shoulders of his worn leather jerkin.

'Fell in the Torridge. Drownded.' His face was expressionless as he sucked on his pipe.

'My God! She's never spoken of it.'

'That be Cook.'

Faith resumed her beating as Cook bustled into the kitchen, little Eleanor running behind clutching her skirts. She looked at this irascible woman with new eyes, with a clearer understanding.

'Now you run along, my beauty, back to your mama, while I get dinner ready. It be getting on for 11 o'clock, according to the sun. I'll fetch your jam tarts out when they be cooked and you shall have one for your puddin'.' A big beam replaced the usual set lips and beetling brow on her broad face as she looked down at the little girl.

Lady de Bere was ringing the bell for dinner. 'Hold on! Us be coming,' protested Cook, bending red-faced by the oven to take out her magnificent herring pie. Faith had already set out plates and cups and cutlery on the long, highly-polished table in the dining room, along with a flagon of Lady de Bere's favourite elderflower wine, a black-jack of cider for the men and boys and a jug of fruit syrup for the girls. She now crossed the passage between the kitchen and dining room carrying the sliced pie and Joseph followed with bowls of peas and potatoes.

The dining room was shadowy as North Hill House faced the wrong way for catching the sun and the walls were of dark wood panelling. Lady Elizabeth de Bere sat at the head of the table, her back to the window, her hands folded in her lap resting on the soft fabric of her gown. Her fair hair hung in ringlets round her full, pale face and was pinned at the back of her head in a bun decorated with a pink ribbon to match her gown.

On her left sat her two daughters, Eleanor, propped up on a cushion so that she could reach the table, and Susannah who was ten and had left behind the innocent charms of childhood. She was a pretty girl, with her mother's fair skin and blue eyes, but a hardness was developing behind the doll-like exterior and she was learning to perfect a condescending curl to her lip.

On Lady de Bere's right was Miles, her second son aged fifteen, who was already starting to imitate the insolent stare and superior manner of Wreford, his elder brother, though his eyes were a warmer, darker blue. Next to him sat a tall, slim young man in his early twenties. This was Stephen Metherell, the children's tutor. He spoke in a quiet, cultured voice and had the long, expressive fingers of a musician.

'I understand Her Majesty is despatched safely to France?' he enquired of Lady de Bere as Faith served the fish pie.

'Yes, indeed. My husband and son helped deliver her into the hands of Prince Maurice and she has set sail from Falmouth.' Lady de Bere looked round the table, smiling at her children. 'I have had a message from your father and, God and rebels willing, he and Wreford will be returned to us here tomorrow night.'

Faith felt herself break out into a sweat and her hand trembled uncontrollably, fumbling with the fish slice. She delivered Master Miles's portion of pie with a thump on its side and he tut-tutted in her ear in his patronising way. She managed to serve everyone else without mishap and was glad when she was able to escape back to the kitchen to compose herself.

TWO

~~~~~

Wreford sat in the Arscott Arms at Chapmans Well on the Launceston to Holsworthy road with his father, General de Bere, and a group of Royalist soldiers. They were breakfasting on bread and cheese and slices of cold meat washed down by mugs of ale. The low-ceilinged room was full of tobacco and woodsmoke and the rumble of male voices. News had just come through that Barnstaple had been recaptured by the rebels, while the men from the garrison were away escorting the Queen to Cornwall, and the men were planning how to take the town again for the King.

Wreford wiped his mouth with a lace-edged handkerchief, leant back in his chair and sighed. He switched his mind off from the talk of battle that surrounded him and looked across the room at the barmaid. When he caught her eye, he winked and signalled to her to come and refill his tankard. She scurried over straight away, bright-eyed and pink-cheeked, and, as she leant over to pour his ale for him, it was all he could do to restrain himself from reaching out to fondle the plump pair of dumplings that appeared to be struggling to break free from her bodice. With his father sitting alongside, he had to content himself with bestowing upon her his most brilliant smile and gently patting her bottom to suggest what might have been.

'Can I do anything else for you, sir?' she asked, looking suggestively out of dark brown eyes into his pale blue ones.

'Sadly not, for the moment,' he replied quietly and, with a pert toss of her head, she moved away among the tables refilling tankards and flirting with the men.

Wreford had noticed the comely wench behind the bar when they had arrived from Launceston the night before. He was going to suggest she join him upstairs later, when her duties were ended, until he found he was to share a room with his father who was such a boring old stickler for correct behaviour. Wreford went out very late, under the pretext of getting some fresh air, hoping to find the maid and a quiet spot somewhere but she was nowhere to be seen. Grinding his teeth with frustration, he returned to bed and tried to get some sleep.

He would be glad to get back to Torrington. The expedition to accompany the Queen from Exeter to Falmouth had been extremely tedious. General de Bere considered it an honour to have been asked to aid and protect the sovereign but Wreford regretted the lack of any real action. There had only been the odd skirmish with isolated bands of rebel soldiers who were easily crushed. Nothing dangerous or exciting. Henrietta Maria was a whey-faced creature who prattled on in French and, although Prince Maurice gave the impression of liking a good time, there was no opportunity for Wreford to find out with his father around.

At least back in Torrington he had a certain amount of freedom and the pick of the local young ladies. His father could not dog his every step and his mother was always understanding. There was that kitchen maid with the pious name and the chestnut hair whose look of defiance he found so provocative. She had proved stubborn so far but he would break her resistance eventually. If all else failed, there were the women of easy virtue in the bawdy house in New Street who were always pleased to see him.

───⁂───

'Now, Faith, make sure you keep a look-out for any rebel soldiers who may be hereabouts.' Lady de Bere shook her blond head in dismay, her ringlets dancing and slapping her cheeks. 'There's no telling what riff-raff might be abroad.'

After checking once more that Faith knew what she was to purchase at the market over in Torrington, she swept out of the kitchen, her silk gown swishing on the stone floor.

'She doesn't tell me what I must do if I should happen to meet a rebel soldier,' Faith remarked, gathering up her basket and putting the coins her mistress had left on the table into her little draw-string leather purse. 'I'm not even sure what one would look like.'

'Don't be insolent to your betters, maid,' admonished Cook, briskly chopping herbs with a sharp knife. 'Everyone knows they have cropped hair up around their ears. That's why they be called "Roundheads". Now, stop your cackle and be off with 'ee!'

Faith set off along the drive of North Hill House to the road which led away down to hill towards Torrington. It was good to be able to stride along freely and easily in her soft leather shoes as there had been no rain for a while and the roadways were dry. When it was wet and the going muddy, she was obliged to wear her pattens to keep her up out of the mud. They were rigid wooden overshoes and the iron hoops underneath were murder to balance on up and down the steep hills to Torrington.

It was a beautiful summer's day, hot and hazy. The sun's heat was tempered by a gentle breeze which freshened her face and played about her neck which was bare under her coif.

Generally, she would have relished an outing to market on such a day, calling in to see her mother, meeting acquaintances in the town and thinking herself lucky that she could return to a fine house when she saw the cramped cottages and dark tenements in which most people spent their lives. But today she felt uneasy. It was not the thought of stray Roundhead solders that worried her but of Wreford de Bere, son and heir to her master, the General, who was returning home today.

He was, at eighteen, only two years older than Faith, tall, confident, fair haired, handsome – and she loathed him. In company he was polite and especially charming to the ladies, who flocked around him eagerly, but beneath the attractive exterior ran a streak of ruthlessness and even, she suspected, cruelty. She had caught a glimpse of this in an occasional flash of his pale, almost translucent blue eyes.

She felt chill suddenly and looked up to see if a cloud was obscuring the sun but, no, the sky was an unbroken blue and in the lane, sheltered by banks and hedges where bees droned and butterflies fluttered amongst the stitchwort and campion and a little blue and yellow titmouse hopped amongst the twigs, it was quite close.

Faith knew Wreford had his eye on her. She could feel him watching her when she was waiting at table, or bringing in flowers for her mistress to arrange. One evening he caught her in the dark corridor between the kitchen and the dining room. He forced hard lips and a raking tongue upon her mouth and clasped her body with rough hands. Her struggle and attempts to push him away only seemed to inflame his ardour.

Suddenly, Cook had called for her. Never had Faith been so happy to hear her bellow and she was able to break away from Wreford and stumble into the kitchen. She could hear him chuckling softly as she made her escape.

'Where've you been, maid? You're all red and flustered. Get thee here and help stir this broth.'

' 'Twas the young master, Wreford!' Faith blurted out, wiping the back of her hand roughly across her mouth. 'How dare he?'

Cook took no notice. All her attention was on the meal she was preparing, trying to ensure all the food was ready at the right time. Faith said no more. From then on she scarcely felt safe moving about the house when Wreford was at home. Many nights she slept with a chair up against the door of her attic bedroom so she would wake if he tried to come in. Thankfully, so far he had not.

Oh, why let thoughts of the hateful Wreford spoil such a lovely day? Faith swung her basket to and fro and burst into song. That always cheered her up. 'Come shepherds, deck your herds!' she sang out, startling a sheep who was peering through the hedge and lumbered off on thin legs to the safety of her companions.

As she came down the steep hill, and the lane turned slightly, a view of Torrington sprawled over the hillside opposite opened out before her. The tenements in New Street edged the horizon like a row of jagged teeth with the higher canine of the church spire over to the right. The thatched cob cottages of Mill Street snaked down from the town to the river almost as if they had slipped down the hillside.

Above the houses of Mill Street a movement caught Faith's eye. She knew, although she was too far away to see him clearly, that it was her father, Peter, flinging lengths of woollen serge over racks to dry. It was one of his tasks to bring the scoured serge up from the fulling mill by the river and to stretch it out on wooden racks on the south-facing hillside to dry in the sun and catch the prevailing wind which swept along the valley from the west. It was hard physical work, to which the firm, knotted muscles in his arms attested, but he was not a man to complain. He preferred working out in the open air to being shut inside soaking the serge in urine and then soaping it before it went for fulling. On the days when he had that job he would come home nauseous from the smell and find it hard to stomach his supper.

Faith came down to the little cluster of cottages which made up the hamlet of Taddiport at the foot of the hill and passed the old leper hospital of St Mary Magdalen. There had been no lepers there for many years now although her parents remembered two or three living there and working their strip fields when they were children.

Faith walked over Taddiport Bridge and paused for a moment to look down at the water rushing below between the arches. Her father had told her it was on its way to the sea and she tried to imagine the place where river and ocean met.

Climbing the cobbles of steep Mill Street she realised how warm she had become with walking. Her woollen skirt was hot and scratchy against her legs and she dreamed of ripping it off and continuing merely in her undergarment feeling the warm sun and gentle breeze caress her bare legs. But such freedom would be short-lived. As like as not, she would be reported to the Constable for unseemly behaviour and clapped in the stocks in the town square to be ridiculed and pelted with rotten fruit and vegetables.

A little way up the street on the left, a cottage door stood open to let in the sun. After rapping briskly on the sturdy wood, Faith stepped over the threshold into her parents' house. Her mother, seated as ever by the hearth, looked up, squinting, to focus on her.

'Faith! Is that you? The Lord be praised to see you fit and well. Help yourself to some fruit cup on the table there. I just have to finish this seam.'

Faith sat at the table and watched her mother bending over the glove she was sewing. Her fingers moved swiftly and deftly, her eyes peered in the gloom. Faith looked around at the pressed-earth floor, the open fireplace where the logs were not lit at present, and the row of tallow candles on the mantelpiece. Two wooden chairs either side of the hearth were where her parents sat and under the window was a wooden chest which had been her favourite place to curl up when she lived at home. Her mother's prie-dieu, where she knelt for her daily devotions, stood up against one wall, a large Bible resting on the shelf, open at today's chapter.

On one side of the hearth, winding stairs led up to two bedrooms while, on the other, a door opened into the kitchen at the back of the house. Beyond there was a patch of garden, closed off from the common land which swept up the hill behind the cottage. This garden was her father's pride and joy where he lovingly grew rows of vegetables to supplement the family diet and the odd row of flowers, though his wife felt these were frivolous and, in some way, unjustifiable. However, there was no doubt that she gained great pleasure from a bowl of daisies or roses on the parlour table, which did much to brighten up the dark little room, and she was pleased to be able to take a bunch of flowers to decorate the church.

'Mother, why don't you sit in the doorway where the light is better, or even out in the sun where it's warm?' The room's earth floor and bare cob walls always ensured a damp chill, especially when the fire was unlit. But Sarah Holman was a proud, private woman.

'I don't wish to be seen working out in the street, thank you very much. Anyway,' neatly biting off her thread, 'I've finished this glove now. That's another pair for Rebekah to take with her tomorrow.' She slapped the finished glove palm to palm with one in her lap and, getting up rather stiffly, she added it to a pile on the table.

Sarah Holman was one of many outworkers who made gloves for Tapscott & Sons. An army of women hunched over their needlework in cottage rooms all over town and out in the surrounding villages to a radius of thirty miles. She gave the finished products to her second daughter, Rebekah, who worked in the factory up in New Street.

Suddenly, a shadow darkened the doorway and Faith's youngest sister, Naomi, skipped into the room. She grinned with delight at seeing Faith and gave her a quick, fierce hug. She was breathless and had obviously been running. She turned to her mother who was packing away her sewing things - scraps of leather, scissors, needles, thread, a silver thimble that had been her mother's – into the oakwood box where she kept them.

'I've just seen our Rebekah with a young man! She

introduced me to him, he's called William.'

'William!' Sarah echoed softly, sinking back into her chair, her eyes misting over. William was the name of the first-born son she had lost and whose death had overshadowed all their lives.

THREE

❦

Faith left for market before her mother had the chance to become maudlin. She had heard the sad tale of her brother's death, aged four in an outbreak of the plague in 1626, so many times she could not bear to hear it all again. It was not that she was without sympathy for her mother's loss and sadness but many people lost children, often more than one, and Faith felt her mother should be thankful for those she had remaining. At least she had other children, unlike Cook.

Faith supposed, also, that she resented her brother William for what his death had caused their mother to become – a rigidly religious woman – and the fact that it was she and her brother and sisters who had to bear the burden of her unwavering fervour.

Their names reflected their mother's religious preoccupation and Faith was sure her father had had no say in their choice. Sarah had named her second son after her favourite prophet, Amos, her first daughter simply Faith, and the two youngest girls were given biblical names, Rebekah and Naomi.

So many Sundays Faith had been obliged to accompany her mother to church, morning and evening, to sit for hours at a time on a hard pew in the chill gloom listening to the ranting sermons of the Reverend Theophilus Powell. He would warn his congregation, in increasingly strident tones, of the terrible prospect of everlasting hell if they did not repent, repent, repent! Faith would leave the church after the service feeling thoroughly depressed and beaten down like a child constantly bullied and chastised. She would look up at the sky and breathe the fresh air with relief. But her mother would seem uplifted by it all and in a kind of smiling trance. She would look younger and less strained so Faith could imagine her prettiness of former years.

Working at North Hill House had freed Faith from enduring those Sunday services and she went only occasionally these days. The de Beres went each Sunday up over the hill to the church at Little Torrington, which lay a half mile or so south of North Hill House, but the servants were not expected to attend. The de Beres were happier for them to stay behind to prepare the family's Sunday dinner.

Faith climbed up the steep street and nodded good-day to the old folk sitting outside their front doors, the women sewing or knitting, the men sucking on clay pipes and watching the world go by through rheumy eyes. She narrowly missed a drenching as a woman threw a pail of slops out of an upper window and a tow-haired child floated a feather in the murky water as it trickled down the edge of the street. A man bumping a handcart full of vegetables over the cobbles touched his forelock in greeting.

She was out of breath when she reached the top of Mill Street and glad to sit for a few moments on the edge of the well at Windy Cross. A woman she knew by sight was winding up a bucket of water and trying, at the same time, to prevent her small boy from climbing up onto the wall. Faith lifted him onto her lap so he could watch the bucket appear without falling into the well.

'There are Roundheads in the area, I'm told,' she said.

The woman grunted with the effort of hauling her wooden bucket over the edge of the well and set it down at her feet.

'I've not seen any hereabouts. Mind you, Roundheads, Royalists, what's the difference if they be billeted on you, eating your food, tramping through your house? Or garrisoned outside town commandeering animals and arms, filling up the inns and rampaging drunk through the streets at night? I'll be glad when the conflict's settled, one way or t'other, so's we can get on with our lives.'

Faith watched her set off down Mill Street, staggering slightly with her slopping burden, her little boy clopping along beside her in his wooden clogs, clutching her skirt, looking back at Faith once or twice. She waved to him and walked on down South Street from where she could hear the tradesmen's shouts in the square.

Farming folk came into town from the countryside around to sell their produce. Those who arrived the earliest secured the best pitches and each vied with the other to call out the loudest.

'Rosy red apples! The sweetest you'll find!'
'Fresh cut flowers, buy a bunch for yer missus!'
'Luv'ly parsley!'

Farmers' wives set out their eggs and cheeses and home-baked pies and pasties on trestle tables and gossiped to each other in between selling their wares.

Fishermen from Bideford and Appledore and as far away as Hartland came to sell their slippery, shining, pungent catch. There were chickens crammed into crates, pecking and clucking, rabbits huddled in boxes, wide-eyed and quivering, and a rough-looking man with a litter of puppies of indeterminate breed tumbling around his heels.

North Hill House sustained itself largely with beef and lamb from its own animals, slaughtered on the farm by the herdsman, Martin Slee. There were eggs from the hens, milk and cream from the cows, fruit from the orchard and vegetables from the kitchen garden tended by Walter Davey with help from old Joseph. However, today Lady de Bere had a fancy for some pork so, as no pigs were kept at North Hill House, Faith made her way down a narrow alleyway beside the Town Hall to a courtyard known as the Shambles where all the local butchers had their stalls. The heat and smell in this enclosed area was quite overpowering and Faith worked her way round looking at the meat, trying to find which was protected most adequately from the flies.

A group of people was gathered around Harry Huxtable's stall, where there seemed to be some sort of commotion, and, as Faith approached, she could hear the butcher's coarse voice bellowing. Curious, she pushed her way through the throng and found the butcher glaring and shouting at Maurice Bosanquet, the Huguenot weaver who lived in a cottage on North Hill just above Taddiport.

'What seems to be the matter, Master Huxtable?' Faith enquired, raising her voice to be heard.

The butcher turned his impatient, mocking eyes on her but she fearlessly stood her ground.

'This furriner don't understand the King's English.' He nodded towards the Huguenot and then shrugged, holding his ham-like hands palm upwards as he looked around in mock dismay at the people gathered in front of his stall.

'I don't think shouting louder and louder will make him understand any better,' Faith countered and, turning towards the Huguenot, she asked, 'What was it you were wanting, Master Bosanquet?'

He looked at Faith part angry, part amused as the other customers pressed close, heads cocked, mouths open, not wanting to miss any part of the exchange.

'Mouton. Mutton, mademoiselle.'

'Some lamb, Master Huxtable, if you please,' Faith said, enunciating every word very clearly and deliberately. The butcher gave her a look which said, 'You'll keep,' and then turned his attention to which joint the Huguenot required.

When the meat was wrapped in a piece of waxed paper and paid for, the Huguenot nodded briefly to Faith and slipped away through the crowd. He was barely out of earshot when the butcher, arms akimbo, addressed the group around his stall in a loud voice.

'Bloody furriner, coming here expecting us to know what he'm on about in that Frenchie tongue!' He shook his head and wiped blood-stained hands on an already gory apron. His customers nodded their agreement and laughed contemptuously.

Looking at Harry Huxtable's large, red face, like one of his own sides of beef, and the ignorant human sheep clustered round his stall, Faith felt a tide of anger rise within her and break suddenly, preventing her from keeping silent.

'You seem to forget, Master Huxtable,' she said, in a clear ringing voice, 'that Master Bosanquet is a craftsman and, if it wasn't for his help, your daughter would still be a third-rate weaver with her cloth full of knots!'

She derived great satisfaction from seeing the

butcher's jaw drop open in astonishment. He was lost for words and, before he could think of any, she turned on her heel and marched off, head held high, accompanied by murmurs from the crowd of 'Well, really!', 'Did you ever?', 'Who does that maid think she is?' Faith was relieved to be out of that stinking place and back amongst the more agreeable smells of fruit and flowers and hot pies in the square. The pork was quite forgotten.

After buying some spices and sugar and other items that her mistress had ordered, Faith treated herself to a custard tart from the stall of a plump, rosy-cheeked farmer's wife. She bit into the soft egg custard, savouring the tang of nutmeg sprinkled on the top and the firm enclosing case of pastry which melted in her mouth. Instead of returning the way she had come, she walked out onto the Commons which sloped down steeply to the River Torridge.

She could see North Hill House standing almost at the top of the hill opposite. It was in the shade as usual for, facing north, it caught very little sun save in the early morning or on summer evenings. Looking across at the house, Faith felt if only she could lift her arms and float on the wind, like the soaring buzzard that was wheeling lazily over the valley, she could be there in moments. As if in answer to her daydreaming, a sudden gust of breeze billowed out her skirt and almost pushed her off balance. Would man ever invent the means to fly? she wondered. It seemed impossible to imagine. Anyway, she would have to trudge down the hill along the narrow paths between the ferns to the river and then climb, panting, up the hill on the other side.

As Faith brushed away the last of the pastry crumbs from around her lips with the back of her hand, a flash of rusty-red up ahead where the pathways forked caught her attention. She wondered what it could be and quickened her step. When she reached the spot where her path joined another which meandered back along the steep hillside by a lower route, there was nothing to be seen. What was it that had caught her eye? Too big to be a bird, too bright for a fox, she had a strange feeling it had been a scrap of clothing, a swirl of skirt but, as she gazed along the narrow grassy pathway, there was no sign of human life. Mystified, she walked on down the hill and crossed over the river. Nobody was stirring in the sleepy little cluster of cottages at Taddiport.

Up the steep winding lane that led to her master's house stood North Hill Cottage, more substantial than those down below. It was here that Maurice Bosanquet lived. He had brought with him from France skills in weaving far in advance of those of the local weavers and he had helped improve the quality of the cloth made in Torrington. It was Faith's father, Peter, who had introduced him to the local weavers but, although they recognised his skills, they had never fully accepted him. Local people were suspicious of anyone from outside. A Cornishman was considered a 'furriner' and not to be trusted so a Frenchman had little hope of a welcome. Maurice Bosanquet lived alone in his cottage with his loom and, for the most part, was shunned like a latter-day leper.

As Faith passed his cottage, the door opened and he called to her. She approached, slightly unnerved by his stern expression but, as she drew nearer, he smiled his sudden warm Gallic smile which transformed his face. 'Thank you for your help at the market, mademoiselle.'

'Don't mention it, Master Bosanquet. I hope I didn't embarrass you. That was not my intention.'

'Not at all. I was grateful.'

'You don't want to worry about Master Huxtable. He's an ignorant man.'

Faith suddenly clapped her hand over her mouth. 'My lady's pork! I forgot to buy it!'

The Huguenot allowed her to leave her basket at his house while she set off back to market, trailing up the steep hill in the heat and dust to purchase the meat. She took care to avoid Huxtable's stall.

When she finally arrived back at North Hill House, it was the last straw for Faith to find Wreford in the kitchen. He was perched on the corner of the table chatting to Cook.

'Where on earth have you been?' demanded Cook as Faith dumped her basket down on the table.

'I forgot the meat.' Faith was in no mood to be conciliatory.

'Her mind was clearly on other things, Cook!' Wreford grinned mischievously at an indignant Cook and then turned to Faith and deliberately looked her up and down with his cold blue eyes.

'I must wash. I'll be back to help you with supper.' Faith turned away from Wreford's intrusive stare and ran up the back stairs to fetch the pitcher from her room and fill it with water from the pump in the yard. As she cranked the handle, she glanced over at the stables where she could see her brother busy with the horses. They all needed attention after their trip to Falmouth.

Faith felt refreshed by a wash and her hair re-done, but weary. When she returned to the kitchen she was relieved to find Wreford no longer there and was soon busy carrying out Cook's orders to help prepare supper. Tonight there was salmon caught from the Torridge only that morning by the estate steward, Hugh Mortimore, and Cook had encased it in elaborately plaited pastry. Faith podded peas, shredded cabbage and peeled potatoes to accompany it.

Supper was a lively meal. Her ladyship and the girls asked about the Queen, how she was dressed and what she was like. Stephen and Miles asked about the journey, whether any Roundheads were encountered and what sort of man Prince Maurice was. General de Bere, usually rather distant and withdrawn, became quite animated as he recounted their experiences. Nobody took much notice of Faith serving although Wreford managed to run his hand down the back of her thigh as she was alongside him. Inwardly she was seething but outwardly she showed no reaction.

It was dusk when Faith went out into the yard to feed the hens. The dipping sun had left a pale yellow glow in its wake in a delicately turquoise sky and long dark clouds lay like distant headlands in aerial shores. Horses snuffled in the stables and a blackbird plunk-plunked its warning call from a bush.

As she crossed the yard, she heard a footfall behind her. Someone in boots was trying to step lightly but, even so, she heard a heel scrape the cobbles. She had no need to turn to know who it would be and, having hastily scattered the corn, she started to run towards the stables hoping her brother, Amos, would be there. There was no sign of him. She suddenly remembered his saying he had to take some of the horses to the blacksmith straight away, so worn were their shoes. In a blind panic she ran up wooden steps to the hayloft above the horses' stalls. As she crouched in a corner trying to conceal herself, she thought, What a fool I am! Wreford would easily find her here. There was no other way out and no-one would hear her if she screamed.

FOUR

Faith was shaking with fear. She tried to compose herself and think of a way out of her dilemma, but failed. She strained to hear Wreford's footsteps on the wooden stairs but there was no sound. Perhaps he had not yet realised she was up here and was looking around the stables below. It was only a matter of time.

Suddenly, she felt a rush of hope. Was that the thud of horses' hooves she could just discern on the night air? Was it Amos returning? Then she realised that the thumping in her ears was her own heart-beat. Her tongue clove thickly to the roof of her mouth, bereft of moisture.

'Faith!' Wreford called impatiently from below. She froze, pressing her back against the rough cob wall, fiercely hugging her knees up to her chest, willing him to go away.

'Faith!' he shouted louder, a rough edge of anger to his voice. 'I know you're in here. Don't play games with me!'

Then everything happened at once. She heard his

footsteps begin to mount the stairs to the hayloft and, in her utter panic, was horrified to feel herself wetting her undergarments. She was about to cry out when she heard a clatter of hooves in the yard, a jingle of harnesses, a snorting of horses, and her brother calling 'Whoa there! Steady now!' The footsteps on the stairs halted and Wreford uttered a low curse. She listened intently, hardly daring to breathe.

'Can I help 'ee, sir?' Amos's slow, mellow voice enquired from the doorway to the stables.

'I've come to see if my horse is ready yet. I need to go into town.' Wreford's voice betrayed no lack of composure.

' You won't find him in the hayloft!' Amos chuckled, allowing himself a rare jibe at his master. 'I have him out in the yard, newly shod. He's been ridden hard, that one, and rightly needs a rest.'

'Well, he won't be getting one this evening. Get him saddled up right away.' Wreford strode out into the yard.

Faith waited until she heard him ride away and then she got up and brushed the straw from her clothes and attempted to smooth down her skirt. She wrinkled up her nose in disgust at the rancid clingy dampness of her underclothes. Her legs were shaky with relief as she picked her way across the hayloft and down the steps. Amos was talking to the horses in a low voice as he led them to their stalls and gave them hay by the light of a lantern he had hung from a beam.

He turned, apparently without surprise, at the creak of the wooden stairs.

'Why, sister, what are you doing up there?'

The homely familiarity of his deep voice, his friendly rugged face and unruly brown hair caused a sob to rise in her throat and she flung herself at her brother, hugging him fiercely. He stood, bewildered, gently patting her back and murmuring, 'There now', until she had calmed down.

Finally, she took a deep breath and stepped back from him. 'I was trying to escape from that slimy toad.'

'Master Wreford?' He smiled slightly at her turn of phrase.

'Who else?'

Amos's lips tightened but he did not question her further. He knew his master's character and suspected that his sister had experienced some problems with him.

'No need to worry about him how. He has gone to console himself with the whores in New Street.' Only the vigour with which he flung down some hay for one of the horses betrayed any emotion.

Faith wished, in some ways, that he would leap on his horse and gallop off in pursuit of Wreford to defend his sister's honour but she knew that was not his way. He liked a quiet life, not argument or confrontation. He was happy here at North Hill House. He loved the horses in his care, found the General to be a strict but fair employer, was comfortable in his own room over the stables and always had plenty to eat. He would not be willing to jeopardise his situation by impulsive actions which would be doomed to failure and he knew he would never get the better of Master Wreford in an argument.

Faith planted a kiss on her brother's stubbly cheek. 'I'm so glad you returned when you did!' Amos smiled affectionately at his sister as she gathered up her skirts and he watched her run across the yard to the pantry door. He wondered what would become of her. She was an attractive maid with that mane of chestnut hair and those striking green eyes. He could see how her youthful freshness and innocence combined with the challenge of her direct glance would inflame the passions of the likes of Wreford and part of him feared for her. However, although she was a mere kitchen maid, she had spirit and strength of character. She would not let herself be downtrodden by anyone, whoever they might be, and Amos was confident that she would be all right, that no harm would come to her.

Faith awoke the following morning feeling light of heart. The horror of the previous night's events had faded with the darkness and only the chair propped against the door reminded her how frightened she had been. She flung back her bedclothes and sprang out of bed, pattering barefoot across the floorboards to stand at her small, high window to see what kind of day it was.

She looked out across the de Bere parkland and rolling fields towards Torrington which was bathed in sunlight. All she could see of the town was the slated church spire and the chimneys of tenements in New Street which were catching the sun. It was a beautiful blue-skied summer's day which matched her mood perfectly. As if in agreement, a thrush puffed out his speckled breast and fluted a lyrical melody from an oak tree near the house. Faith looked towards the distant coast but there was a slight haze and she could not see the glint of the Ocean this morning.

Down in the kitchen Cook was full of the latest news which she was imparting with great relish to Hugh Mortimore and Joseph. The estate steward was a wiry little whippet of a man with a sharp, weather-beaten face and surprisingly large, gnarled hands. Both he and Joseph were seated at the table enjoying mugs of ale.

' 'Tis Thomas Monck,' declared Cook, more than ready to repeat her story for Faith's benefit or, indeed, for any newcomer who cared to listen, 'nephew to our mistress's brother-in-law, General George Monck. Killed last night at midnight, he were, in South Street by men from his own company. Mistaken password, they say. Couldn't see who it was in the dark. Must've thought he were a Roundhead strayed over from Barnstaple.'

Faith did not know the gentleman involved so this news was merely a matter of curiosity to her and not of any particular sadness. It did nothing to dispel her feelings of well-being which were further enhanced by finding Wreford not in for breakfast. In fact, only the General and Stephen Metherell were in the dining room when Faith entered with a tray of ale and cold meat and cheese. As she set the leather-jack before her master, his young daughters appeared. 'God save you, Papa,' they chorused as they slipped onto their chairs and arranged their skirts. 'And you, my children,' he looked up briefly from the news sheet he was perusing and smiled at them in his kindly, distracted way. Faith returned to the kitchen to fetch their bread and milk and to see if there was any strawberry conserve in the pantry.

'My lady has gone already to Potheridge to offer comfort to her sister, Lady Monck, and her husband, the General.' Cook was still in full flow having, no doubt, repeated her story right from the beginning for the benefit of Amos who had joined the other men for a mug of ale and a hunk of bread and cheese. He looked enquiringly at Faith as she passed by on her way back to the dining room and winked in answer to her smile.

Master Miles had appeared at the breakfast table by this time and was deep in conversation with his tutor about the Norman invasion of Britain in the eleventh century on which he was currently writing an essay.

'Did you know, Master Metherell, that our family the de Beres are descended from the Normans?' he was asking, a somewhat haughty expression on his young features.

Faith barely had time to gobble her own bread and cheese, washed down with hasty gulps of ale, before the bell tinkled from the dining room signalling for her to come and clear the table. As she swilled out the leather-jack and pewter mugs and rinsed crumbs off the dishes at the kitchen sink, the sun shone obliquely through the window in front of her and Faith's high spirits spilt over into song:

'Early one morning just as the sun was rising,
I heard a maid singing in the valley below:'

Her voice was clear and true and surprisingly strong. Joseph stood alongside and nodded his grizzled head in time to the tune as his knobbly old hands fumbled with a drying cloth and plates.

'What a caterwauling!' exclaimed Cook as she thumped her wooden spoon round a mixing bowl. 'What's a body to do to get some peace and quiet around here?'

'Take no notice, maid,' Joseph croaked into Faith's ear. 'Her's jealous. Can't tell the difference between a pretty song and a boiling pan. Her's tone deaf!'

Faith laughed and continued her song with even more gusto:

'O, don't deceive me, O never leave me!
How could you use - - -'

Suddenly, the door from the hall opened with a crash. Faith turned to see General de Bere standing in the doorway. She could not remember his ever coming to the kitchen before.

'Who is it singing?' he asked, in stentorian tones.

'I tried telling her, sir - - ,' Cook began.

' 'Twas me, my lord,' Faith spoke up without hesitation as she turned to face him, wiping her wet hands on her apron. 'I'm sorry if I was disturbing you.'

The General looked at her as though seeing her for the first time. 'On the contrary. I can't remember when I heard a lovelier sound, especially welcome on a day of sadness in the family.'

He stood unmoving for a moment gazing at her as if unsure what to say next and, with the servants likewise immobile, watching him, formed an involuntary tableau. 'You are Sarah Holman's daughter, are you not?' he asked her, finally. 'I think I detect a certain likeness.'

'Yes, I am, my lord.' Faith was rather taken aback, wondering how the General should know her mother. Then she remembered that Sarah had also been kitchen maid for the de Beres many years ago when she was a girl and the General a young man. It was she who had begun the connection between their two families.

'We shall be entertaining the General and Lady Monck in a few days' time,' the General continued. 'They will need a diversion and some music would do very nicely. Would you sing something for them accompanied by Master Metherell on the harpsichord? I shall ask him to arrange it with you.' Without waiting for her reply, he turned on his heel and left the room as swiftly as he had arrived.

Faith, Cook and Joseph stared at each other, bemused. 'He liked the caterwauling,' Joseph cast a sly glance at Cook.

'Don't you be getting ideas above your station, maid,' she warned, resuming her vigorous stirring.

Faith remained gazing at the door through which the General had departed, her thoughts racing. She had never sung in public before. Would she be nervous? What would it be like to perform with Master

Metherell? Would they be well-received - - -? Out of the mass of anxieties and speculation tumbling around in her head, the sole question to come to her lips was, 'What on earth would I wear?'

FIVE

Stephen Metherell politely stifled a sigh when General de Bere put to him his proposal for the entertainment of his grieving kinsmen. He had no interest in teaching songs to ignorant maidservants or in performing with them in front of the nobility.

'Could I not just play General and Lady Monck some pieces on the harpsichord?' he ventured, but his employer was adamant, his mind made up.

'No. A few songs will be more cheering. The maid has a most striking voice. Have you heard her sing?'

'No, sir, I can't say I have.'

'I would be much obliged if you would arrange things with her. Half a dozen songs will do nicely. Perhaps a couple of suitably melancholy pieces but some merry ones as well.'

'Very good, sir,' Stephen agreed in a resigned voice as his master turned away and marched out of the library with a heavy tread.

Oh, how unspeakably tedious! He could not even remember what the wench's name was. To him, she was merely a pair of hands placing food and drink in front of him. Except for that one occasion. He felt his face flushing, even now, remembering.

She had been wearing her hair in a long thick plait hanging down under her little white, lace-trimmed coif and, as she turned away from setting his meal before him, it swung out and the end caught him on the cheek. He had exclaimed in surprise and indignation and the whole family had laughed at him. The girl apologised, when she realised what had happened, and he remembered the look in her eyes as he glanced up at her. Not at all contrite or properly cast down. Instead, they were dancing with merriment as she looked directly and fearlessly at him. He felt she had somehow got the better of him.

Sighing again, Stephen got up from the table and made his way through the drawing room to the hall. As there seemed no way of avoiding the situation, he had better arrange a time to meet the girl before Master Miles turned up for his Latin lesson.

He pushed open the heavy door into the kitchen and found himself in a world of warmth and delicious smells, busyness and noise. It was so different from the chill quiet of the rest of the house that he simply stood motionless in the doorway for a moment, taking it all in. The enticing aroma of newly-baked bread mingled with the tang of coarse tobacco. The cook was a vision in white cap and apron with an aura of flour floating around her as she thumped her rolling-pin back and forth upon the wooden table top. She was haranguing an old man who was perched on a stool by the hearth and seemingly unperturbed by the tirade as he puffed contentedly upon his long clay pipe. The cook had to raise her voice over a clatter of pots and pans coming from the sink where the girl he had come to find was scouring out a large conserving pan.

Nobody had seen him or heard him arrive above the din so he announced himself by clearing his throat decisively, 'Ahem!' and three faces turned towards him: the old man's wrinkled, nut-brown cheeks and solemn watery gaze, the cook's broad, flushed face, her mouth gaping open mid-sentence, and the girl, sharp-eyed, enquiring.

It was to her that he addressed himself in his most formal manner. 'The General has asked me to arrange a meeting with you to discuss the singing of some songs. I propose 3 o'clock this afternoon in the library.'

Faith had turned from the sink to face him. She was inwardly amused by his evident lack of composure and immediately felt more at ease herself, banishing earlier worries. 'Certainly, Master Metherell,' she smiled at him. 'General de Bere did mention it to me the other day. I'll be there, if that's convenient with Cook.'

She looked over at Cook who was clucking her tongue in disapproval. 'Ridiculous, if you ask me! Servants performing before their betters!' she declared, shaking her head. 'Still, if that's what the master wants, who's us to argue? Joseph'll have to do your jobs for you.' Her lips were set in a tight line as she resumed her thumping and rolling.

'The maid's got a beautiful voice,' piped up the old man in a smoky croak. 'Sweet as a lark.' He nodded to himself as he turned back to the glowing embers and drew on his pipe, savouring the strong tobacco.

'Till 3 o'clock then?' Stephen confirmed with Faith, who was still looking and smiling at him with a somewhat disturbing intensity, and he backed out of the kitchen feeling strangely awkward. He found himself wondering whether they were talking about him as soon as he had gone and, if so, what they were saying.

He returned to the library and found Master Miles waiting there for him with his Latin books. He forgot everything else as they proceeded to unravel the intricacies of Caesar's Gallic Wars.

Faith had never taken much notice of Stephen Metherell. Just as she had been merely a pair of hands serving food to him, so he was an indistinct figure attached to the de Beres to her. She knew nothing of his origins. His voice possessed traces of the local Devon burr but far less pronounced than her own. He was obviously well-educated to be employed as a tutor by a family such as the de Beres and she had the impression he was not at ease among servants.

At dinner time that day Stephen was the only male at table as General de Bere had taken his two sons and the dogs off hunting. Faith snatched a few glances at him in between serving slices of hot roast beef and pouring ale. She was trying to gauge what sort of person he was so that she might know how best to approach him. She realised that he was doing the same as their eyes met more than once. His were solemn with no spark of sympathy or friendliness and Faith felt he eyed her as a farmer would a calf at market or a lady would a piece of porcelain, estimating its worth.

It was with a certain trepidation that she prepared to meet him that afternoon. She washed her hands and splashed her face at the pump out in the yard, after having cleared away all the dinner pots and dishes. She tucked some stray wisps of hair under the edge of her coif, took off her apron and hung it behind the pantry door, straightened her bodice and smoothed down her grey woollen skirt. She crossed the hall silently in her soft leather slippers and hesitated before the drawing room door to see if she could hear anyone within. Hearing no sound, she tapped gently on the partly-open door before peering round to make sure her lady was not sitting in there working at her tapestry. The room, though south facing, was dark from the trees and rising ground outside the window, and empty. Faith hurried across the room to the library door and knocked upon it more confidently than she felt.

'Come in!' a light male voice called and, entering the library, Faith saw Stephen seated at a harpsichord near the window leafing through sheets of music. She had seldom been in this room and gazed in awe at all the books lining the walls. Deep recessed windows with seats looked out across parkland and let in rays of afternoon light.

'What a lovely, friendly room!' she burst out and Stephen smiled at the natural spontaneity of her remark. His smile altered his face completely, banishing the bleak, disdainful look and making him seem far more approachable and friendly. Faith felt encouraged.

'The General tells me you know 'Early One Morning' and he would like that included in our performance. Do you know all the verses?'

Faith had come to stand facing him across the harpsichord. 'Yes indeed, Master Metherell, I have sung it since I was a child.'

'Let us begin with that one then and see how we get on.' He looked down at the keyboard, glad to escape from the intensity of her green eyes, and played an introductory phrase.

Faith cleared her throat and ran her tongue around her lips which had become dry all of a sudden. She was nervous for a moment but once she started to sing she relaxed and enjoyed the familiar song. She kept her eyes on Stephen's face but only once did he look up at her. That look, however, was sufficient to let her know that he was surprised, and impressed.

Stephen could not believe what he was hearing! What a voice! What clarity and strength and unwaveringly accurate tuning! When she had sung all four verses and he had played the concluding chords, he put his hands in his lap and forced himself to look at her. He was lost for words and only managed to mutter, 'Very good, very good.' Then, realising how inadequate this was, he added, 'You have a lovely voice, Faith.' He coloured slightly as he called her by her name which he had learnt from Master Miles that morning.

'Why, thank you kindly, Master Metherell.' Was there a hint of mockery in her voice? He could not be sure. She looked guileless enough.

'Perhaps you could sing the last verse a little more quietly? I think that would be most effective.' She sang the verse again, as he suggested, and he nodded, satisfied.

'Do you know 'Drink To Me Only'?' he enquired, pushing back, with a nervous gesture of his long-fingered hand, a lock of brown hair which insisted upon flopping down over his forehead. 'It's a particular favourite of Lady de Bere's.'

'No, I can't say I do.'

'Well, I'll play it to you and then, perhaps, you will try the tune to 'la'.'

She watched him as he played the song which sounded to her rather like a hymn. She noticed the way his light brown hair fell about his shoulders, the errant lock slipping forward once again. She saw how his long eyelashes fanned out across his pale cheeks, how his nose was straight and rather elegant and his mouth serious.

Faith only had to sing the tune through two or three times and she knew it. She had a good ear and Stephen had to admit that what he had expected to be a chore was becoming quite a pleasure.

'I'll teach you the words now.'

Faith moved round the harpsichord beside him. 'If I stand here, I can learn them for myself.'

'You can read?' Stephen looked up into her face, his mouth hanging open in amazement as she nodded.

'My mother taught me so that I could read the Bible. She's a very religious woman,' she added, as though by way of explanation.

Stephen felt quite light-headed and wondered what other surprises this serving girl had in store for him.

They finished by singing 'Now is the Month of Maying' and Stephen harmonised in his light tenor voice in the refrain. They watched each other as they sang to keep in time with the 'fa la las' and, in a pause between verses, they were suddenly interrupted by the cheery chirruping of a robin perched on a bush just outside the window. It threw them completely and they both burst out laughing which finally broke the reserve between them. Faith thought how nice Stephen looked when he smiled and he wondered how it was he had never really noticed this girl before with her dancing eyes and beautiful voice.

'Mother, is there any way you could make me a dress if I can obtain some material?' Faith was on her way to market in Torrington the next day.

'No child. Not for the day after tomorrow. I have a consignment of gloves to finish and, anyway, how would you afford material?' Her mother peered at her from the hearth where she was stirring a stew in a black iron pot suspended over the flames.

'I had hoped Master Bosanquet might be able to get me some and I could pay him weekly.' Faith had lost enthusiasm for the scheme as soon as her mother had refused.

'You don't want to be indebted to foreigners,' Sarah Holman stirred her stew with increasing vigour.

'Really, Mother, you sound like Harry Huxtable!' Faith was unable to hide her irritation and gathered up her shopping basket.

'You know I don't hold with singing in public,' Sarah continued, as if determined to have the last word.

Faith knew full well. When she was a child and had sung about her chores, Mistress Tucker next door had often remarked that she could be a professional singer one day. But Sarah would have none of it. She believed that prancing about on stage with people ogling you, as she put it, was the way to ruin. The only public singing she approved of was in church.

'I'm to sing in General and Lady de Bere's salon, Mother, not an ale house,' Faith said testily as she made for the door.

'Well, you'll have to ask her ladyship for help with a dress in that case,' Sarah retorted.

Faith paused in the doorway before leaving her parents' house and looked back at her mother bent over her cooking pot. She sighed and asked, 'Why can't you ever be pleased for me?'

SIX

Wreford stood in front of his looking glass and gazed at his reflection. He was pleased with what he saw. His silky fair hair hung to his shoulders where it curled slightly. He had recently cultivated a moustache and a small pointed beard after the style of King Charles in his portrait by Vandyke and Wreford felt this facial hair gave him an air of maturity and authority. His mother was particularly taken with it.

He straightened the sleeves of his deep blue velvet doublet and fluffed out the lace frill at the wrist of his silk shirt. His breeches were of the same material as his jacket and fitted just under his knees. They combined elegance with comfort. He smoothed out a wrinkle in his pale blue silk stockings and made sure the large bows on his shoes were tied securely. Then, after a final appraising glance at his overall appearance, he made his way downstairs to the salon.

Wreford had very little interest in the coming soiree, expecting it to be a thoroughly dreary affair, but his parents had insisted he be present out of respect for his aunt and uncle. He had only met their nephew, Thomas, once or twice years ago but, in his view, anyone who managed to get himself shot by his own men must be an idiot. However, his tolerably attractive cousin, Catherine, would be there so he could amuse himself with her.

He was also, he had to admit, rather curious to see how the little kitchen maid acquitted herself. She was always worth looking at and he was interested to see her in one of his mother's old dresses.

Lady de Bere had been most put out about the whole affair at first. 'I don't hold with servants performing in front of their masters,' she had declared one evening at the supper table. 'The girl might not behave appropriately and embarrass us all! Then what would my sister and her husband think of us?'

'She is only to sing some songs, my dear, of which she is perfectly capable. We're not expecting her to make polite conversation all evening.' General de Bere looked in amusement at his pinkly indignant wife.

'And she had the temerity to ask me what she should wear! She said she didn't have anything suitable. What does she expect me to do about it?'

'I'm sure you must have an old gown she could use,' suggested the General.

'A servant! Wearing my clothes?' Lady de Bere looked about to burst with indignation.

'Your old, cast-off clothes, my dear.' The General was beginning to lose patience with his wife. 'Would you rather she appeared before our kinsmen in her cap and apron?'

'I'd rather she didn't appear out of her normal role at all,' retorted his wife but the General had his way, as Wreford knew he would.

In the salon Wreford poured himself a goblet of Canary wine from a carafe on the heavy oak sideboard and walked over to one of the tall windows that looked out across the sloping parkland and fields. One day all this will be mine, he thought, and, tipping his head back, downed his wine in a single draught. Having poured himself another, he strolled across the room, his footsteps muffled by the thick Turkey carpet, and stopped before the huge stone fireplace above which hung a portrait of Charles I. Wreford was to meet the King shortly at Crediton and he wondered what kind of man he really was. His slim pale face and the angle of his eyebrows gave him a somewhat melancholy air. He was said to be a good horseman, a talented painter, temperate with food and drink and very devout. Wreford suspected he was a stiff, proud, restrained man and not nearly as much fun as his nephew, Prince Maurice. Still, he was the King, divinely appointed, and, for that alone, commanded his subjects' devotion. Wreford longed to be out on the battlefield proving his own allegiance to his sovereign.

The General and Lady Monck and their daughter, Catherine, arrived looking like a group of crows in their mourning. The General was a large man with a strong, heavy face and black hair falling in thick waves to his shoulders. His wife, Anne, was plump and fair like her sister, Lady de Bere. Catherine, a slim, rather pale creature, had pinned a red rose at her bosom and looked not at all sad. Wreford smiled at her for her small act of defiance and noted the glint of mischief in her prominent blue eyes as she walked towards him.

After their meal the whole family and their guests returned to the salon and sat in heavy leather chairs which had been placed facing the harpsichord which stood between the two windows. Susannah and little Eleanor had been allowed to stay up and listen to the music and they sat on stools at their parents' feet.

Before seating himself, General de Bere rang a small, tinkling bell on the mantelpiece and, after a brief pause, the door from the library opened and Faith entered with a swish of pale green silk followed by Stephen. They curtsied and bowed to their audience and Faith looked a little overawed as she stood facing her employers and their guests while the tutor took his place at the harpsichord.

'Faith! You look beautiful!' Eleanor's little voice piped up unselfconsciously before being hushed by her mother and Faith flashed a smile at the child. It seemed to relax her and, when Stephen had announced the title of their first song and nodded at her to begin, she opened her mouth and sang as though she had been performing in front of people all her life.

Wreford could not take his eyes off her and neither, he noticed, could that pansy of a tutor. She looked magnificent in the gown his mother must have discarded for being too tight. It fitted Faith perfectly revealing smooth creamy shoulders and the gentle rise of her young bosom and defining her neat waist. Its pale colour complemented her rich chestnut hair, half of which was arranged in a bun on top of her head while the rest cascaded gleamingly down her back. Wreford had never seen her before without her coif. He was finding it hard to pay due attention to Catherine and that young lady became increasingly petulant and demanding, whispering to him, plucking at his sleeve. What a silly creature!

The evening's entertainment was deemed a success and even Lady de Bere had to admit that her husband's idea had been a good one. 'If manners maketh the man, then it's equally true that clothes maketh the woman,' she had twittered in a piercing voice during a lull between two songs. 'Faith could almost pass for a lady in that old dress of mine.'

Faith was pleased and relieved that the evening had gone well. However, apart from enjoying a warmer relationship with Stephen, nothing changed in her situation. Not that she expected it to. Next morning, after her brief moment of glory, she was back to being kitchen maid once again. On the go from dawn to dusk and beyond, at everyone's beck and call. If ever she sat down by the kitchen fire with a mug of ale she could guarantee her mistress would call her for something, or the children would need to be seen to, or her master would require his boots polishing, or Cook would want her pudding stirred.

Shortly after the concert, however, Faith had the prospect of an easy day when all the family were out. She determined to make the most of it. Lady de Bere had been up early calling for her clothes and for Faith's assistance to get her into them. This was usually the task of Jane, her personal maid, but Jane had been taken ill and retired to her bed. 'Truly,' Faith said later to Cook, 'I don't know whether my lady's been indulging in too many pastries or whether she's in the family way again but it was hard work buttoning her into her dress this morning!' Her mistress was displeased about it and took out her frustration on Faith by speaking sharply to her. She gathered up her daughters and Miles and drove off to Great Potheridge to visit her sister for the day.

General de Bere was up and away early as well, taking his elder son with him. Faith heard him shouting to Amos to ready the horses and there was a great neighing and stamping of hooves out in the stable yard. Men from the locality who formed the General's militia were gathering to accompany him and Wreford to Crediton, some thirty miles distant, where King Charles was reviewing his army gathered there by his nephew, Prince Maurice. There was a great feeling of excitement amongst the men and voices were raised in shouts and laughter as they clattered over the cobbles and away down the drive. 'I'd have liked to've seen the King,' Joseph said, wistfully, gazing out of the window at the departing riders but he was too rheumaticky to sit on a horse now.

Faith went to feed the hens, sneaking a hunk of fruit cake from the pantry on her way out. First she made sure that Cook, who was boiling broth, had her back turned, otherwise she would have got the rough edge of her tongue.

Outside she shivered as she scurried across the yard with her bucket of grain. A surprisingly chill wind streaked across the hills from the west and swept around the corner of her master's house. The birds in the rookery were flapping and cawing, their harsh cries competing with the whoosh and swish of the wind in the trees.

Faith collected what eggs she could find and, walking back to the house, a movement caught her eye and she spotted a lone figure trudging along the drive towards her. Curiosity, and the unhurried nature of her day, made her shelter in the lee of the house and watch the stranger's approach. It turned out to be a woman in a dark red skirt, tall of stature with a swing in her step, nobody Faith knew. She saw the coloured kerchief round her head, the thick dark braid of hair, the flash of silver earrings and the dark eyes with a knowing look set in a weathered face.

'No tinkers here!' Faith admonished her, stepping out from her sheltered place. 'Away! Be gone with you!' What a sense of power she felt, speaking to her so!

Usually it was she who was ordered about all day.

The gypsy did not turn and scurry off, as Faith had hoped, but came closer and gazed at her. Faith noticed that her eyes were hazel flecked with a curious yellowy-green. Her stare was too strong for Faith who had to look away.

'Beware of pride, my child,' the woman said in a deep, clear voice with á rich West Country burr. 'Treat others as you would wish to be treated, not as you are treated.'

Faith shifted uneasily from foot to foot feeling rather foolish. 'What do you want, anyway?' she asked, embarrassment making her voice a bark.

'I have clothes pegs, fresh purple heather and lucky silver charms,' said the gypsy, stirring the contents of the flat willow basket that hung from her arm and lifting out a sparkling trinket that she dangled before Faith's face. Faith looked at it, almost hypnotised by its swing and shine, and heard the woman whisper, 'I think you'll need some luck before this day is out.'

Faith's unease turned to anger. 'Be off! Away with you! A serving girl doesn't have money for such things and General and Lady de Bere are out so you'll have to go elsewhere and frighten other folk with your superstitious talk,' and, tossing her head, she flounced off round to the side door and in through the pantry to the kitchen.

There was only Faith, Cook and Joseph for lunch and Cook did them proud. They tucked into succulent pork pies, large slices of fruit cake (Faith kept quiet about her earlier piece) washed down with cider made with apples from their master's orchard.

Afterwards they dozed companionably round the kitchen fire. Cook was snoring slightly, though she would never admit it, and Joseph lit and puffed on his old clay pipe.

Gradually, Faith became aware of a distant, insistent sound getting ever louder. It was the clop of horses' hooves and the clank of arms and armour approaching up the drive.

'The master's back sooner than expected,' she said, as they heard shouts and commands out in the yard.

Joseph got up creakily from his stool and hobbled across the kitchen to peer out of the window. His jaw dropped, letting his pipe shatter in shards on the stone floor, and his voice was barely more than a cracked whisper when he announced: ' 'Tain't the master! It be Roundheads!'

SEVEN

Robert Armitage sighed as he shifted his position in the saddle to ease a stiffness in his backside and pushed a lock of dark curly hair out of his eyes. His lobster-tailed helmet seemed to weigh particularly heavy today and he was sweating under his steel breastplate.

He leant forward and patted his chestnut horse roughly on the neck. 'Good old Trooper,' he murmured, 'you've done me proud, lad.' Trooper kept plodding on, merely flicking his ears in recognition of his master's voice. He was a big, solid, workmanlike animal, not swift or graceful but steady and strong. He had carried Robert faithfully for many a mile and brought him safely out of some tight spots, including one on Hatherleigh Moor that very morning.

Robert was part of the Earl of Essex's Parliamentary army which, after abandoning an attempt to capture King Charles at Oxford, marched to the West Country to recapture the ports of Devon and Cornwall and to relieve Plymouth which was constantly under siege.

They spent over two weeks at Tiverton and managed to take Barnstaple as a large portion of the garrison were withdrawn to escort the Queen into Cornwall on her return to France. However, the fort at Appledore, which dominated the Taw and Torridge estuary, remained in Royalist hands.

Essex held a council of war at Tiverton to decide whether to turn back and face the challenge of the King's forces, which were marching into Somerset, or to advance further west to the relief of Plymouth. He took the latter course of action and the Parliamentary army made its way through undulating countryside to Crediton. From 'Kirton', as the locals seemed to call the place, they moved on to Bow, Okehampton and Tavistock. Essex found a lot of local support for the Parliamentary cause but he was hampered by a lack of arms for his new recruits. He also found that many Devonians refused to be led by regular army officers and would only follow locally prominent gentlemen.

Finally, five miles west of Tavistock, the Parliamentary army marched in buoyant mood into Cornwall. They were a considerable body of men, including nearly two thousand horse, and came from all parts of England. They were from all walks of life, speaking in a variety of regional accents, and were united simply by their desire to see a fairer government of their country than the tyranny of a King who seemed to be becoming increasingly out of touch with his people.

Local folk were gathering in the harvest from the fields and they often stopped and straightened up from their labours to stand, mouths agape, to watch this great body of men marching through the countryside. Sometimes the army came up against caravans of up to ten little horses laden with corn tied onto racks, balanced on either side of their backs, supported by two people walking alongside. It would have seemed easier to use carts but these little goonhillies, or gunnellies, were too small to pull a cart. When the narrow lanes were blocked by a line of gunnellies with their teetering loads, a lot of shouting would ensue and manoeuvring into adjoining fields.

Once in Cornwall, Essex realised his situation was hopeless. His army found itself caught between the combined forces of Charles and his nephew, Maurice, which were regrouping at Exeter, and the Royalist forces of Cornwall under Sir Richard Grenville. After suffering defeat at Lostwithiel, Essex ordered his body of horse to escape while he surrendered his foot-soldiers and, humiliated, withdrew to Plymouth. There was constant movement of cavalry across Devon for more than a week as fleeing Parliamentarians tried to avoid contact with Royalist garrisons and search parties. Some sections of the Parliamentary horse went to Plymouth, the majority went to Crediton, Barnstaple and on to Taunton, while one body of horse went to Tavistock and came under attack from Lord Goring's men.

Robert was with a body of some six hundred men who made their way up over the edge of Dartmoor to Okehampton. Here the land opened out and was reminiscent of Robert's native Yorkshire. He felt he could breathe more easily here after the deep, damp stony lanes sheltered by hedges and trees where you only got occasional glimpses of countryside through gateways. They took a northerly route from Okehampton and were trailing disconsolately and wearily across Hatherleigh Moor when a Royalist troop came rushing out of nowhere and routed the tired and hungry Parliamentarians, chasing them for miles in different directions.

Robert thought with regret about the blow he had

delivered to the Royalist in the plumed hat. His sword had caught the man's face, though he had not intended it. If he had not struck out, he himself would have been slain. He had turned and seen the man approaching at a gallop, sword raised, just in time to defend himself. However, the memory of the shocked expression and spurting blood on the man's face, as he reared back and tumbled from his horse to be trampled under Parliamentary hooves, would stay with Robert for a long time. He did not relish hand-to-hand fighting but was prepared to do what was necessary.

'By God, we were lucky to escape with our lives!' declared George as he rode up alongside Robert. He spoke in a broad cockney accent and his ruddy face was shiny with perspiration.

'Aye, we were,' Robert agreed. 'We left a good many comrades dead on that moor.' They trotted on in a reflective silence for some way, unusual for George who generally had more than enough to say. Predictably, it was he who eventually broke the silence.

'This campaign's been a bloody disaster right from the start. We should never have let the King leave Oxford and certainly not allowed him to join forces with Prince Maurice. That's a hell of a lot of Papists to have at your heels. Then, of course, it was bad luck to come up against that bastard, Grenville, in Cornwall - - -'. He rambled on not seeming to expect any reply from Robert who merely smiled, or nodded, or sometimes furrowed his brow in an expression of doubt at some of George's wilder statements. Mainly, he was simply relishing the fact of still being alive, content to look about him at the rolling countryside and trying to ignore the gnawing hunger in his belly.

The sun had left its hottest station immediately

overhead and was starting its gradual slip away to the west when a dozen or so exhausted horsemen straggled up over the hill by Little Torrington and saw North Hill House nestled amongst its sheltering trees. A flash of red caught Robert's eye and he saw a handsome gypsy woman standing motionless by the roadside, a basket of trinkets over her arm.

'Who lives in the big house yonder?' he asked her, noticing the greeny-hazel eyes in the leathery nut-brown face.

'General de Bere,' she replied with a Devonshire roll to her Rs, 'loyal supporter of the King,' she added meaningfully, a ghost of a smile playing around her lips.

'No hope of victuals for us there, then,' George grimaced, ' 'tis only to be expected hereabouts.'

'The General and his men and the lady of the house are all abroad today, there are only servants at home,' the gypsy added.

'Thank you for your information, ma'am,' said Robert, wondering for an instant whether they were being led into a trap, but something about the steadiness of the woman's gaze made him think not. He and his companions turned into the drive leading to the house, looking about them warily. Suddenly, a magpie crossed their path in a flash of black and white, uttering its raucous, rattling cry.

'One for sorrow,' intoned Ralph, a poor-looking bony fellow with blackened teeth. The men looked at each other, some in alarm, some amusement. Then a second magpie hopped out from under the bushes in pursuit of its mate and Ralph grinned gappily. 'Two for joy. We'll be all right then!' The men laughed more loudly than was necessary and relaxed.

Joseph was still gazing open-mouthed out of the window and Cook, rudely awakened, had stumbled to her feet and was smoothing her apron and straightening her cap when the heavy knocking came at the door.

'You'd best open up, maid,' she said to Faith who, heart pounding, made her way through the pantry.

They looked a fiercesome bunch, eyes shaded by the peaks of their helmets, dirty blood-smeared faces divided in half by the protective spikes which jutted out over their noses. They strode past her into the kitchen in their heavy spurred boots and made themselves comfortable at the table or stood propped up against the walls. They pulled off their helmets and dropped them, clattering, onto the floor.

'Something to eat and drink, if you please,' Robert addressed Cook.

'And plenty of it, we're starving,' piped up George, winking at Faith as she made her way to the pantry to fetch black-jacks of ale. 'You're a pretty one to be sure, miss,' he said to her as she returned and placed the ale before him. Joseph gathered his wits sufficiently to push tankards and cups onto the table while Cook, her lips tight with fury, hacked bread and cheese and fruit cake into hunks and piled them onto plates which she set before the men with a series of thuds.

The kitchen was filled with the stench of hot leather and sweat and metal and echoed to the harsh sound of the men's voices in a mixture of accents Faith had never heard before. Some of them she could barely understand. She watched them from a distance, standing over by the hearth, and thought they looked less frightening without their helmets. Only a couple of them wore their hair cropped up around their ears and not all, as Cook had led her to believe. Some of them were, in fact, not unpleasant looking. It was obvious, by the way they fell upon the food and drink, cramming in great mouthfuls of bread and cheese and cake and gulping noisily, that they had not eaten for some time. Faith wondered what made men support the rebel cause but, looking at them, realised they were not monsters but ordinary human beings.

'Some more ale over here, missy.' George waved a leather-jack in the air and, as Faith took it from him, patted her smartly on the bottom. She dared do no more than glare at his red, sweaty face and marched off to the pantry.

'We'll sleep well tonight, though I'd sleep better with a wench like that beside me!' George's eyes were feverish from the ale as he leered at Faith who carefully put down the filled jack at a distance from him.

'For pity's sake, George, leave the lass alone!' said a deep, firm voice with an unfamiliar pronunciation and Faith looked gratefully at the speaker, noting his thick curly black hair that tumbled onto his collar and his friendly dark eyes. She briefly smiled her thanks and Robert's grin was swift in response, a flash of white teeth against brown skin.

'We must be on our way if we're to make Barnstaple before nightfall,' said Robert finally and, with a collective moan, the men gathered up their helmets and trooped out into the yard. Robert nodded his thanks to the three servants, his gaze lingering longest upon Faith who returned his look directly and fearlessly.

The men watered their horses at the trough by the stables before riding off along the drive. The sound of their horses' hooves was barely out of earshot when a mighty shout arose from the lane and the crack of gunpowder and the clash of steel reached the ears of Cook, Joseph and Faith who stopped still in the midst of clearing up after the Roundheads.

' 'Tis the master and his men returning from Crediton,' said Cook, with a nod of satisfaction. 'They've arrived just in the nick of time to see off those rebels!'

EIGHT

Sarah Holman had asked Faith to accompany her to evening service at the parish church. Her husband, Peter, had been called away to help sort out a crisis at the mill. Rebekah had to work extra hours at Tapscotts to help finish a special assignment of gloves. Sarah was angry that her daughter should be expected to work on the Sabbath but knew that to refuse might cost Rebekah her job and her wages were a great help to the family. Naomi was at her aunt's house in Calf Street for the day to help amuse her young cousins.

It was still warm as Sarah and Faith walked slowly up Mill Street but Faith carried her shawl over her arm for later on. Sarah bade her neighbours 'Good evening' as they passed and took hold of Faith's arm for support when the street reached its steepest part.

Inside the church the chill air and deep shadows induced in Faith the usual feeling of despondency. Sarah found space for two on the end of a pew towards the front. She immediately sank to her knees on the bone-numbing stone floor in prayer and pulled Faith down beside her. No wonder her legs have difficulty getting up Mill Street if she spends long kneeling on this cold floor! Faith thought irreverently. She resented her mother presuming to control her actions but did not wish to cause a scene in the church by refusing to kneel. She rested her hands on the back of the pew in front and her forehead upon her hands and wondered what to pray about. Merely parrotting an oft-repeated verse seemed so meaningless.

Suddenly, she found herself thinking of the group of Roundheads who had invaded the kitchen of North Hill House a few weeks back. In particular, she recalled the man who had spoken up on her behalf and looked at her with interest as he departed. Although he could hardly be called handsome, with his dirty, unshaven face, there was something very attractive about his shining dark eyes and ready smile. Had he been one of those pursued and struck down from their saddles by General de Bere and his men and left to lie injured and dying by the roadside up towards Little Torrington? It was her brother, Amos, and Hugh Mortimore who had had the task of taking the dead in a cart to the graveyard. Faith realised her fists were clenched as she offered up a fervent prayer that the dark, curly-haired Roundhead had got away safely. As she opened her eyes and sat back on the hard wooden pew, she found her mother was already seated. Sarah gave her daughter a fond smile and an approving nod.

The Reverend Powell was at his most thunderously impassioned that evening. Faith found his manner of preaching tiresome to such an extent that it distracted her from what he was actually saying. She glanced at her mother who was gazing at the vicar with rapt attention. She looked about the church, watching the dancing shadows against the walls created by the guttering candles standing on the window ledges, and let her mind wander.

She was thankful when the sermon finally came to an end and the congregation rose to its feet to sing a hymn before the final prayer and blessing. The hymn was a favourite of Faith's: 'Let us with a gladsome mind, Praise the Lord for He is kind:' and she sang out with gusto. The most uplifting aspect of church services was, in her view, the singing when the sound of people's voices swirled around the high walls and pillars echoing up in the lofty arched ceiling; it was then, she felt, that one was nearest to God.

It was dark when Faith and her mother stepped out onto the cobbles of the churchyard and a shadowy figure appeared at their side.

'Mesdames Holman, would you care to share my light on your way home?' It was the Huguenot weaver holding up a flickering lantern.

'Why thank you, Master Bosanquet. Most kind, I'm sure,' Sarah replied, somewhat archly Faith thought. She and her mother fell into step beside the Frenchman and set off for home by way of the town square.

Men were still lounging outside the Black Horse with tankards in their hands. Several of them were unsteady on their feet and raucous of voice. 'Drinking on the Sabbath!' Sarah snorted in disapproval as she passed by. This was one matter upon which she was in agreement with the Puritans.

A belligerent voice rose louder than the rest and called after them: 'Hey! Mistress Hoity-Toity, who's no better than she should be, for all her airs and graces and religious ways.'

Faith recognised the voice as belonging to Huxtable the butcher and turned to call a sharp response but

Sarah caught hold of her arm and hurried her around the corner into South Street. Faith shook her arm free impatiently, irritated with her mother for controlling her actions a second time that evening. She was about to complain but one look at the set expression on Sarah's flushed face and the presence of Master Bosanquet made her change her mind.

'An unpleasant man, Huxtable,' the Frenchman remarked, politely attempting to break the awkwardness between the two women.

It was only later, when Faith thought back to the scene and recalled the butcher's words, that she realised, with something of a shock, that he had not been speaking of her as she had assumed. Those last two words of his, 'religious ways', clearly referred to her mother. Whatever had he meant?

'How is it that you attend our church, Master Bosanquet?' Sarah enquired as they walked up South Street past the Mayor's house and into a freshening breeze. Faith was glad of her woollen shawl and crossed it tightly over her chest. 'Are you not a Papist like the Queen, being French, as she is?'

Faith's insides curled up in embarrassment. Her mother did have this unfortunate tendency to sound sharp, accusing. Master Bosanquet did not seem in the least put out. Perhaps, as a foreigner, he was unaware of subtle nuances of tone.

'I am a Protestant, Mistress Holman. This is why I came to England. Life is not easy for a non-Catholic in France. One is always watching one's back, suspicious of people, having to justify one's actions. No-one knows what the new king, Louis XIV, will do in the future regarding the Huguenots. He is still but a child and who knows how he will be advised?'

'But it's not easy for you here, is it, being a foreigner?' Faith asked.

'On the whole people leave me alone. It's not so bad. And some people are friendly.' Turning towards Faith, the lantern light caught the angular planes of his face giving him a ghoulish look as he smiled.

They passed the well at Windy Cross and began the descent into Mill Street. It was narrow and winding at the top and their voices echoed between the buildings. The lantern was useful in lighting up their way so they did not stumble on the uneven cobbles of the ill-lit street and it was pleasant to see the faces of people you were talking to but outside the lantern's pool of light the shadows looked blacker and more threatening than usual. Faith was used to walking in the dark, and was not afraid of it, picking her way along the familiar route, her eyes adjusting to the darkness and her other senses alert to her surroundings.

Outside her parents' cottage, further down the street where it widened out, the Huguenot invited Faith and her mother to take a glass of wine with him at his house.

'Thank you, Master Bosanquet, but no. I have things to see to before the morning,' Sarah replied straight away and, turning towards Faith, 'and you had best be returning to your master's house, daughter.'

Faith made no reply but pecked her swiftly on the cheek. 'Goodnight Mother. I'll call in to see you when I next come to market.'

She continued down the hill and over the river with the Frenchman. The cluster of cottages and the empty leper hospital looked more forlorn than ever in the dark.

By the time they reached his cottage the offer of a drink seemed eminently inviting to Faith and she accepted his invitation. It was also partly in defiance of her mother who would have been horrified at her being in the house of a man she hardly knew, unchaperoned, and at this late hour.

He opened his front door with a large key which he took from the pocket of his jerkin. They stepped over the threshold into a tiny entrance lobby with doors on either side and narrow stairs straight ahead twisting away to the upper floor. Master Bosanquet opened the door on the right and led the way into his parlour. As he placed the lantern on the mantel shelf and set about lighting candles, Faith looked about her with interest.

The small room was dominated by a large weaving loom, an intricate structure of wood and taut strings and shuttles and bobbins and an emerging length of cloth of delicate colours. There were windows on three walls which, though small, must have helped with light for his work. On the walls between the windows hung tapestries and, while the Huguenot disappeared into the other room to fetch the wine, Faith had a closer look at them. They were more like paintings, depicting landscapes with rivers, trees and castles, and were intricately wrought. Even in the candlelight Faith could appreciate their richness of colour.

'Are these your work, Master Bosanquet?' she enquired, as he returned carrying a dark green bottle and two drinking vessels of a fragile, transparent material.

'Yes. They are of scenes near my place of birth. They remind me of my homeland.'

'Do you miss it badly?' She had noted a wistful look in his dark eyes but he smiled slightly and shook his head.

'A pretty paysage is not enough to make a home. You need people too. And it is also pretty countryside here.'

'Does the river in your tapestry have a name?'

'It is the Loire, the longest river in France, and there are many magnificent châteaux dotted along its banks.'

'Châteaux?'

'Castles, you say in English. Come and sit over here by the hearth and I shall pour the wine.'

Faith watched, entranced, as the rich ruby liquid filled the transparent goblet. So slender was its stem that she hardly dared pick it up.

'What is this cup made of, Master Bosanquet?'

'It is Venetian glass which I purchased during a visit to Italy many years ago. Wine is better out of a glass than pewter, I find, and I have not acquired a taste for ale, I'm afraid.' He smiled ruefully.

Faith lifted her glass, relishing its fine smoothness against her lips, and tentatively sipped the glowing liquid. It's taste conjured up impressions of mellow wooden casks, smoky fires, sharp vinegar and soft fruits, all somehow mingled together, and she felt a warmth seeping through her body right down to her knees.'

'Vin rouge,' Master Bosanquet said, indicating the liquid.

'Vin rouge,' Faith repeated, trying to imitate his pronunciation.

She felt comfortable with him and found him easy to talk to. Perhaps it was the effect of the wine. They spoke of many things – the wife he once had who had died in childbirth, his escape from France in a small boat, how he found himself in Torrington, her father's help in gaining recognition for his weaving, how he acquired his supply of French wine, the de Bere family – and it was late when Faith finally got up to leave.

'My lady will be waiting for her cup of hot milk. She has one every night before going to sleep.'

'Would you like me to accompany you up to the big house?' he enquired, gallantly, but Faith shook her head.

'No, no, thank you. I'm used to walking these lanes in the dark. Good night, Master Bosanquet.'

'Bonne nuit,' he replied.

'Bonne nuit,' Faith repeated, giggling slightly at her clumsy accent.

He stood at his front door as Faith started up the hill, her legs strangely heavy from the wine. She turned once and waved before he was out of sight in the darkness.

She had just reached the part of the road where it curved left between high banks when she heard the clop of a horse's hooves approaching behind her up the hill. Her heart lurched. Please don't let it be Wreford! There was nowhere to hide in this deep pit of a lane, no field gate she could slip inside. She hurried on as the horse and rider gradually caught her up.

'Why, Faith, you're out late!'

Faith expelled the breath she found she had been holding as the rider jumped down beside her. 'Amos! What a relief!' She chattered on. 'I've been drinking wine with Master Bosanquet out of Venetian glass. He's such an interesting man. Where have you been?' Amos remained strangely silent. 'What's her name?' Faith teased.

He laughed, quietly. 'Margaret. Her father keeps the Barley Mow in Well Street. A comely maid and good company. You shall meet her one day.'

'I look forward to it.' They walked on up the hill to their master's house, mostly in a companionable silence, occupied with their own thoughts.

Stephen had felt restless all evening. He knew Faith often visited her family on a Sunday afternoon but she was usually back by early evening. He wanted to show her a song he had found and thought she might like to sing. If he was honest with himself, he simply wanted to see her and spend some time with her.

He wandered about the house and called into the kitchen several times to check whether she was there. He tried to occupy himself reading but kept finding himself thinking about her and having to read the same sentence over again. When it had become quite late and she still had not returned, a ghastly thought suddenly set his heart pounding. Perhaps she had a young man in the town. He was not sure how he could cope with that.

He finally abandoned any hope of seeing her that evening and retired to his room where he eventually drifted off to sleep dreaming of her. But, as he watched the intimate scene between himself and Faith with that strange objectivity of dreams, his own face changed into that of Wreford as he bent down to kiss her lips. Stephen woke with a start in a sweat and, cursing his own stupidity, tossed and turned, searching for sleep which eventually crept up and overtook him unawares.

NINE

～❧～

It was a September morning of big scudding clouds hurried on by a wind rushing in from the west. Patches of blue sky suddenly appeared and the sun burst through bathing the hillsides in a cheery glow. There was a slight chill in the air, a feeling that the year was turning towards winter, and the first leaves were fluttering down from the trees.

General de Bere had gone off hunting in Kennick's Wood with his kinsman, General Monck. Wreford was not in the mood for hunting, not for deer or foxes, anyway. He was the only male present at breakfast, his brother having gone out early with his tutor to study the local flora, or something equally tedious. He watched Faith as she leant over to pour milk in his sisters' cups and placed a basket of fresh bread before his mother. Her movements were graceful and economical. There was no clumsiness about her.

The sensations which stirred within him at the sight of her reminded him that he must pay a visit to the apothecary. He needed a potion to deal with an unpleasant infection he seemed to have been cursed with. It had been a mistake to go with that new maid in New Street. He thought at the time she had looked none too clean but the tempting curves of her body and the sultry pout of her full lips had been too much for him to resist. He flung his chair back from the breakfast table in annoyance and strode out through the hall into the yard shouting for Amos to bring him his horse.

The sun was intermittently warm on Wreford's back as he rode down the steep hill towards the river. The leaves of a poplar shimmered and swished in the wind like rushing water and a cockerel crowed from a back yard of a cottage in Taddiport. There was little sign of life except for two old men tending their strip fields alongside the river.

Wreford urged his horse up the steep cobbles of Mill Street quicker than was necessary and by the time they reached Windy Cross the poor beast was sweating and heaving. Wreford eased up and let the animal plod slowly down South Street while he looked about to see if anyone of interest was abroad.

His attention was caught by a peal of girlish laughter and, looking towards the imposing entrance of the mayoral residence, he saw a young lady with her maid stepping down into the street. She had flaming auburn hair and a peachy skin and was dressed in finery not often seen in Torrington.

He immediately jumped down from his horse and approached the young lady with a springing step. He swept off his hat and reached out for her hand, bowing low over it. 'Wreford de Bere at your service, ma'am.'

The young lady was not at all discomfitted. In fact, she seemed highly amused, 'Good morning to you, Master de Bere. I am Sylvia Moune, daughter of the

Mayor, and delighted to make your acquaintance.'

Wreford was eager to prolong the encounter and treated Mistress Moune to his most dazzling smile. 'Would you and your maid care to take some refreshment with me? I could secure us a private room at the Black Horse.'

Sylvia made a moue of regret with her naturally curving lips, noting appreciatively his smooth blond hair, penetrating blue gaze and charming smile. 'Thank you, but no. We have to go visiting in Castle Street but I am sure we shall meet again. Perhaps at the fair on the Feast of St Michael the Archangel. I do so love a fair, especially the peep shows and the coconut shies, don't you?'

The invitation was surprisingly direct and Wreford laughed in delight. 'Indeed I do. I shall look forward to seeing you there.'

He bowed once again to the Mayor's daughter, turned and sprang up into the saddle of his horse. He bestowed a further smile upon the young lady and her maid, who was pretty enough herself, and rode off down into the town square with a swagger. He was excited at the prospect of a new affair and all thoughts of the apothecary were forgotten.

When Robert Armitage rode down from Huntshaw Cross and over Darracott Moor he saw spread before him in the sun the market town of Torrington. Approaching from Barnstaple, the town appeared below the rider whereas a traveller from the direction of Exeter would look up and see it perched on its hill above the River Torridge.

Robert skirted round to the left of the town through Hatch Moor. He had no wish to draw attention to himself in what he knew to be a Royalist stronghold. He had enjoyed the invigorating ride over the hills from Barnstaple, with glimpses of the sea in the distance, past sleepy hamlets of cob and thatch cottages which nestled in the folds of the hills or stood on their summits robustly facing into the wind. Several times, though, he had asked himself what he thought he was doing returning to this place. His chances of seeing the girl were pitifully slim and he had no wish for a further encounter with General de Bere and his militia. The Roundheads had lost four of their men in the skirmish at Little Torrington. One of them was George whose ceaseless cheerful cockney chat Robert now quite missed even though it used to madden him at times. Robert hoped he had been laid to rest in a proper way and wondered where he was buried. Those of them who had managed to escape had made their way to Barnstaple under cover of darkness.

He found himself on common land by the river beneath the town and let his horse drink his fill as he leaned against a gnarled oak and thought of the serving girl with the chestnut hair.

The sound of lively chatter and high-pitched laughter interrupted his thoughts and his heart beat wildly with a mad hope that one of the girls he could see approaching might be the very one he was looking for. This was not the case, of course. It was two milkmaids who looked at him with interest as they passed by on the river-side path, whispering and giggling as soon as they were a little further on. He briefly thought of asking them if they knew the servant girl he was seeking but he was wary. He did not want to advertise his presence in this place and the milkmaids did not look the most discreet.

He took hold of Trooper's bridle and strolled along the path which loosely followed the river. A steep hill, on top of which was the town, reared up to his right. The ground was covered with thick green ferns and grasses and pinky-purple rosebay willow-herb whose beard-like seeds were floating away on the wind. Further along, another path joined his from higher up the hillside and he was wondering which way to go when he saw a woman walking towards him with a swift, swinging stride.

As she approached, he remembered seeing her before. It was the gypsy he had encountered near North Hill House. 'Good day to you,' he said, as she drew near and turned her sharp, flecked eyes upon him.

'We meet again,' she greeted him without preamble.

'I am looking for a girl I met when I was last here. She works up at the big house on the hill.' He nodded in the direction of North Hill House which he could just see amongst the trees up on the hill across the river from the town.

'A girl with chestnut hair and a fearless glance?'

Robert smiled. 'The very same. Do you know her name and where I might find her? I mean her no harm.'

The gypsy regarded him steadily and silently for a moment, then she said, 'Her name is Faith Holman and at present she's up to market. If you want to see her you'd best be waiting down by Taddiport Bridge. She'll be returning that way. And there's a bit of shelter amongst the trees on this side.'

Robert bowed his head slightly to her in thanks. 'I'm much obliged to you.'

Suddenly, the woman stooped and picked a bunch of the wild miniature snapdragons which were growing by the path and tucked the tiny delicate flowers into the lacing of his coat. 'For luck,' she said, tersely. 'You'll be needing it,' and she strode off up the steep path leading towards the town. Robert continued along by the river and, when he looked back, she was already out of sight.

He found the clump of trees opposite Taddiport and let his horse graze. He took from his saddle bag a leather bottle of ale and a paper-wrapped parcel containing a dry hunk of bread and some hard yellow cheese. He sat himself down at the foot of a tree, leaning against its trunk, keeping the bridge in view and a wary eye out for any passers-by. The sun was warm in that sheltered spot and, after a while, having quenched his thirst and satisfied his hunger and lulled by the constant murmur of the river, he closed his eyes and fell into a doze.

Faith left the bustle of the market and started back to North Hill by way of the Commons. Ferns brushed her skirts and she stopped every now and then to pluck a ripe blackberry from the tangle of bushes beside the path, taking care to avoid the overripe 'Devil's blackberries.'

She was startled by a woman stepping out in front of her all of a sudden, apparently from nowhere, and Faith recognised her as the gypsy who had called at North Hill House with her basket of trinkets.

'There's a young man looking for 'ee.'

Faith looked at her in horror. 'Not my master Wreford!'

'No, my dear. A dark-haired foreigner, older than you but with no ill-intent. He's down by Taddiport Bridge.' She turned and left abruptly before Faith could question her further.

Intrigued, Faith walked on down the hill towards the river. 'Older than you', 'a foreigner'. Was she referring to Master Bosanquet? But 'dark-haired'? The Huguenot had been dark but his hair was mostly grey now. A sudden wild hope sprang up in Faith's mind but she quickly smothered it. He was either dead or far away by now.

She kept her eyes firmly fixed on the bridge from the moment she could first see it but she could not see anyone there. As she approached the bridge, she looked around but there was no-one. No-one in sight over in Taddiport, no-one in the direction of Mill Street, no-one over by the mill and, turning to look back the way she had come, no-one behind her on the path. Perhaps the gypsy was playing a trick on her to pay her back for her haughty manner at their last encounter?

Then a movement amongst a clump of trees on this side of the river caught her eye. It was a horse grazing. It was saddled and bridled and must have a rider nearby. Cautiously, she retraced her steps a short way. At first she could see no-one and then she realised there was a figure slumped at the foot of one of the trees. Perhaps it was an injured person? Warily, she drew nearer and saw it was a sleeping man. Recognising the tousled dark curly hair, the prominent nose, the firm set of the lips, she blurted out, ' 'Tis you!'

TEN

Robert's eyes flew open and, seeing Faith, he scrambled to his feet, a delighted smile spilling across his face.

'I had feared you dead!' she gasped, only just managing to control an impulse to fling herself at him and give him a great hug.

'You have thought of me, then?' His voice was deep and slow-speaking and he grinned down at her.

'A little,' she murmured, flushing slightly. She thought how horrified her mother would be to see her talking in such a forthright manner to a stranger but she was her own person, old enough to make her own decisions, and she liked him.

'I know your name is Faith,' he said, 'the gypsy woman told me. Mine is Robert.'

'Robert,' she repeated, as though trying it out.

He laughed. 'I love the way you say it, those delicious rolling Rs! Say it again for me.'

She obliged, flushing deeper, and asked him, 'What are you doing here?'

'I came hoping to see you.'

She was quite overwhelmed by the implications of that simple statement, the feeling of responsibility for being the cause of someone endangering himself. 'Where have you come from? I had thought you to be miles away by now.'

'Come. Let us sit down.' He stripped off his heavy buff coat and laid it on the ground. Underneath he had on a shirt of coarse cloth, none too clean, she noticed, and he pushed back the sleeves revealing muscular brown arms.

'I've been in the garrison at Barnstaple since leaving here but I don't know how much longer we'll be able to hold on there. There's talk that the Royalists are regrouping and planning to try and recapture the town.'

'Why are you on the side of Parliament?' she asked, looking at him intently.

His face became serious. 'The King is becoming a tyrant. Every year he demands more and more money in taxes to fight wars he can't possibly win. He must be stopped from ruining England.'

'But he is the King by Divine Right.'

Robert snorted with contempt. 'That's as maybe but he's been abusing his position for too long and needs to be taught a lesson. It is Parliament who will have to do so, by refusing him the money he needs for his wars, otherwise he will bleed the kingdom dry.'

Faith had never heard such talk before and gazed with fascination at his intense expression and flashing eyes.

'I live near Sir Thomas Fairfax and one day I did some carpentry work at his house. Now there's a great man! He supported the King at first but he came to see how difficult life was becoming for ordinary people. He presented a petition to the King on behalf of the

Yorkshire clothworkers who were suffering great hardship and facing ruin. But the King won't see any point of view other than his own. Fairfax decided he could no longer give the King his loyalty and he called out a militia to fight for Parliament. He's a fine soldier and I hope to fight alongside him one day.'

'Is Yorkshire the place where you are from? Is it far from here? Does everyone there speak like you do?'

He laughed at the torrent of questions. 'Aye, I'm from up north, lass, a good four or five days' journey from here.' He emphasised his Yorkshire accent even more, making her laugh too.

'Is the country thereabouts the same as here?' She was curious to know what lay beyond her home valley.

'No. On the whole 'tis more open and wild though I thought on the ride over from Barnstaple how the landscape reminded me a little of home with its wide, sweeping hills. The fields up there are separated by drystone walls and you can see for miles. The weather's colder too.'

Faith suddenly remembered the custard tart in her basket that she had bought for later. 'Are you hungry?'

'I brought some bread and cheese and a stoppered jack of ale, thank 'ee kindly.' The corners of his eyes crinkled up in an appealing way when he smiled.

'Will you have a custard tart? They're very tasty.' Her face was so eager, so earnest, he could have kissed her.

'You eat it.'

'We'll share it.' She tried to break the tart in half but it threatened to disintegrate and lose its filling. He put his large, warm hand on hers to stop her and said, 'Don't wreck it! You start it and I'll finish it.'

She felt oddly shy biting into the soft custard and crumbling pastry and then passing over the remains of the tart to a stranger, the bitten edge frilled with the indentations of her teeth marks, but he took it and finished it as if it were the most natural thing in the world for them to be sharing their food.

They sat there amongst the trees looking at the river and talked about all manner of things. She told him about her family, her life at North Hill House and her singing. He told her about life in the Parliamentary army, the places he had seen during his years marching about England and how he was a carpenter by trade. He conveyed to Faith his love of working with wood, especially making furniture, and said he longed to get back to it. 'One day,' he sighed, 'when this conflict is over.'

Faith enjoyed talking with Robert and felt wonderfully at home with him. It was with extreme reluctance, having glanced up and noted the position of the sun, that she told him she would have to go. 'They'll be asking for me up at the house.'

He got up with her, reached down for his crumpled coat and roughly shook it out before putting it on once more. 'I'll walk with you a way.' He fetched his horse and together they walked on down to the bridge where they stopped and watched a pair of stately swans floating downstream.

After talking so easily together, they found themselves suddenly tongue-tied. Faith was all too aware of the danger he was in and realised that she was unlikely ever to see him again. Robert kept looking at her, savouring her fresh young skin, the scatter of freckles across her small, straight nose and the fearless gaze of her clear green eyes. He, too, realised the transitoriness of this encounter but was determined to rejoice in the fact that he had found her and enjoy the moment for what it was. He did not think about the future.

They were just the other side of the bridge when they heard a clatter of hooves and, turning, Faith saw a rider with unmistakable shining blond hair on a white horse emerging from the end of Mill Street.

'Quick! 'Tis Master Wreford. You must go. I'll pretend to be giving you directions.'

Robert swiftly climbed onto the faithful Trooper and Faith made a show of pointing along the road to Langtree. He gave her a last warm smile before urging his horse away and Faith called after him, 'God go with thee!'

'Who was that you were speaking to?' demanded Wreford as he reined in alongside Faith. She was just leaving behind the cottages of Taddiport and was starting the uphill climb towards North Hill House.

' 'Twas just a traveller, master.' Her heart was beating wildly.

Wreford sat astride his fine horse looking down at her, a mistrustful frown creasing his forehead. 'You appeared to be talking very intently for a casual meeting with a stranger.'

Faith gripped the handle of her basket tightly as she looked up at him defiantly, aware that Robert's safety depended upon her reply. 'He asked me if I knew a family in Langtree called Skinner but I told him the name meant nothing to me.' She shrugged, with studied indifference. 'All I could do was direct him towards the village itself.' Now go away and leave me alone, she added silently to herself.

'Hm. Well, get a move on. Cook will be waiting for your purchases.' Clearly dissatisfied, he kicked his horse and urged him up the steep lane leaving Faith to follow with her basket.

Faith heaved a sigh of relief that he had not dismounted to torment her. She was not to know that his mind was full of Sylvia Moune and the possibilities their next meeting might produce. She wondered where Robert was and turned round, half hoping to see him coming up the hill behind her. He would have to double back from the Langtree road to return to Barnstaple but she dared not wait around now Wreford had seen her and she did not want to put Robert in danger.

There was no sign of Maurice Bosanquet at his cottage as she passed and Faith wondered if he was busy at his loom. When she had drunk wine with him that evening after church he had shown her how it worked and she imagined his slight frame moving to the rhythmic actions of weaving; raising the shafts, flicking the shuttle, lowering the shafts and beating the weft to produce his fine cloth.

The rest of the climb up to North Hill House did not seem half so long and steep as usual for Faith's thoughts were full of her encounter with Robert. Before going indoors, she crossed the yard to her favourite gateway where she dumped her basket down on the ground and climbed onto the first rung to gaze out over the countryside. She could just make out a narrow slice of the North Ocean catching the afternoon sun. She wondered in what direction Robert's county of Yorkshire lay and what it was like to be so far from home.

Cook appeared round the side of the house from the pantry with a bucket which she deposited on the ground with a clang. 'Oh! There you are. Thought you'd left for good!' she snapped, on seeing Faith. 'Throw these peelings to the hens and then get inside, there's work to be done.'

The last day but one of September was the Feast of St Michael the Archangel and it was celebrated in Torrington with a fair. Peals of church bells announced the start of the day's activities and, as soon as he had finished breakfast, Wreford leapt on his horse and rode across the valley to the town.

A continuous stream of men, women and children on horses, on foot and in vehicles of every kind were converging on Torrington. The town was packed and the streets around the square were full of stalls selling all kinds of food and gewgaws. New Street was converted into a cattle market and the windows of the houses were protected with strong posts and bars to prevent damage by the animals penned on the pavement.

Groups of young men were making their way down to the swampy ground at Common Lake for a game of 'outhurling', a rough form of football in which a leather ball was tossed and kicked amongst the many players and the goals were half a mile apart.

Wreford left his horse tied to a post in South Street and tossed a coin to a scruffy urchin in tattered breeches and bare feet with the instructions to watch the animal till he returned. He strolled down to the square, pushing his way through the crowds, and along Castle Street to Barley Grove which was covered with peepshows, coconut shies, boxing booths and shooting galleries.

Wreford wandered around amongst the entertainments unable really to give his attention properly to them. As the day wore on, he felt a mounting impatience, wondering whether Sylvia Moune was going to make an appearance or whether she had quite forgotten their assignation.

He was about to repair to the Black Horse for a jug of ale when he saw her emerging from a peepshow with her maid, both of them convulsed with giggles. He strode over to them straight away, sweeping off his plumed hat and bowing low with a flourish. 'Mistress Moune, how agreeable to see you again!'

'Master de Bere! What excellent timing! We have laughed ourselves silly at a most improper peepshow and now I have a taste for some coconut milk by way of refreshment. How is your aim? Can you topple one for me at that shy?'

Wreford was only too happy to oblige. He offered Sylvia Moune his arm and together they made their way through the throng, her maid trotting along behind. He knocked down a coconut with his second throw and cut the top off for her with the sword he wore at his hip. He watched with amusement as she tipped her head back, drinking with enthusiasm from the whiskery vessel until the thin, white liquid spilled down her chin and she wiped it away carelessly with the back of her hand, laughing up at him with sparkling eyes.

They spent the rest of the day together, lunching at the Black Horse, watching the runners in the 'Round the Tree Race' flying off down the steep part of Castle Hill on their way down to the river and Taddiport where they ran round a tree in one of the fields and then returned, puffing and sweating, up the long paths to the town. They cheered on the men who were slipping and sliding as they tried to climb the greasy pole erected on top of Castle Mound and they laughed at the antics of the crazed cock at the cock-cubbitting. That poor creature, minus its tail, was trying to escape when the earthenware pan it had been placed under was finally smashed by sticks. In a yard just behind the square they came upon a session of bull-baiting and stopped to watch the dogs tormenting the old bull. Men stood around stooping, their heads together, and women joined in holding out their towser aprons to break the fall of the dogs. All of a sudden a jack russell terrier flew up in the air, tossed by the enraged bull, and landed in the apron of Sylvia's maid, Annie, who just managed to hold out her skirts in time. She shrieked as the over-excited animal scrabbled wildly to free itself, trying to nip her as she let it to the ground.

As evening drew on the revel grew noisier. Torches flared, drums were beaten, gongs struck, trumpets tooted and men shouted. Wreford bent to whisper in the ear of his fair companion. 'Could not Annie be sent to ready your chamber for your retiring? I know of a nice quiet spot down beyond Castle Mound where we might sit and watch the last of the sun and be alone for a while.'

Sylvia turned towards him and noted the suggestive gleam in his light blue eyes. She gave him a smile of complicity and dismissed her maid immediately. Then she took his arm once more and they walked swiftly away from the hustle and bustle of the revel to the gathering darkness of the Commons.

ELEVEN

The year 1644 rolled round towards Christmas and Faith was asked to sing at several musical events in the locality, in churches and in the houses of the gentry, accompanied by Stephen on the lute or harpsichord. Lady de Bere was not at all in favour, at first, believing servants should keep to their allotted station in life and not presume to mix with their superiors. However, when local interest was shown in the fact that this girl with the lovely voice was a kitchen maid in the de Bere household, she changed her opinion and decided to bask in the reflected glory of her servant's talent.

They performed some carols at a service in Little Torrington church. Faith shivered as she sang in her best grey woollen dress and her breath escaped from her mouth in billowing clouds along with the words and music. When she returned to her pew, she wrapped herself once more in her cloak to try and keep at bay the bitter December chill. She had noticed the sharp features and alert expression of Maurice

Bosanquet amongst the congregation while she was singing and, after the service, he approached her and congratulated her enthusiastically on her performance. The Reverend Powell from Torrington was also present and he asked Stephen and Faith, in his effusive, overbearing manner, if they would be good enough to grace his own Christmas service with a few carols.

Faith felt rather nervous as she stood to face the large congregation in Torrington parish church but took encouragement from the smiling faces of her family who were sitting near the front. Naomi sat beaming between her parents and Rebekah was alongside with her young man, Will Avery. Next to him was Amos with a comfortably-built, rosy-cheeked girl whom Faith took to be Margaret from the Barley Mow. Peter Holman glowed with pride as his daughter's sweet, strong voice soared up and around the vaulted roof of the church. He noted with interest the way in which the young man who was accompanying her on the lute looked at her every so often but he was unable to tell from his daughter's expression whether or not the feelings he displayed were reciprocated. Even Sarah relaxed and enjoyed the music and was sufficiently moved to offer to make Faith a dress to wear when she sang for her employers and other local gentry. Lady de Bere had given Faith a length of peach taffeta, having decided that it was not a flattering colour for herself, after all.

Sylvia Moune was amongst the guests at North Hill House when Faith and Stephen provided some seasonal after-dinner music for the de Beres. The Mayor's daughter was clearly rapt in Wreford whom Faith thought looked a trifle wild-eyed and feverish. Perhaps he had been a little too free with the wine at dinner. She herself felt like a princess in the peach taffeta dress which rustled as she walked and contrasted very becomingly with her rich chestnut hair, a feeling which was confirmed by Stephen's whispered 'You look lovely!' just before they entered the salon.

They were invited by General and Lady Monck to sing at Great Potheridge where a number of the local gentry were gathered, including Sir Richard Grenville who, with his harsh features and bright red hair, looked most forbidding as he sat scowling. Looking at him, Faith could quite believe the stories she had heard of his ruthlessness and brutality but even he smiled and applauded at the end of their performance.

Some refreshment had been set out for Faith and Stephen in another room. After closing the door of the salon behind them, Stephen took hold of Faith's arm and gently pulled her into the centre of the hall under the chandelier, from which a bunch of mistletoe was hanging, and planted a kiss firmly on her lips which were slightly open in surprise. She blushed with pleasure at this uncharacteristic show of emotion and watched, smiling, as, according to custom, he plucked off one of the white berries. 'Plenty of berries left for more kisses!' he laughed, eyes sparkling.

Faith enjoyed the rapport between herself and Stephen when they were making music together. She was slightly in awe of his knowledge and his ability to coax sweet sounds from the harpsichord or pluck a melody on the strings of his lute with his long, flexible fingers. Mostly, he was very correct and formal with her but the expression she caught in his hazel eyes sometimes as he looked at her, the occasional compliment he paid her and the fervour of his embrace under the mistletoe made her wonder what thoughts and feelings were harboured behind his solemn countenance.

On Christmas Day Faith had to work hard in the

kitchen helping Cook prepare the de Beres' dinner. There was the goose to be basted, vegetables to be prepared, gravy to be stirred, milk to be skimmed for cream to have with the plum pudding, wine to be uncorked and the best plates, cups and cutlery to be laid on the table.

Stephen had a day's holiday to visit his family. He rarely spoke of them but Faith had discovered that they lived at a place called Clovelly, a village tucked into a steep, narrow cleft in the hills which led down to the sea on the North Devon coast. He had an older brother who was a fisherman like his father. Faith had the impression that he was slightly ashamed of his humble origins and, though she could understand it in an ambitious young man eager to better himself in the world, it was not one of his characteristics she admired.

Faith was allowed a holiday on Boxing Day and, together with Amos, walked down the hill to her parents' house carrying boxes of food left over from the de Beres' Christmas dinner: slices of cold goose, with potatoes, carrots, cabbage and a bowl of Cook's herb stuffing to go with it, as well as a large portion of plum pudding, a dozen mince pies and some apples.

'So generous of the General and Lady de Bere!' exclaimed Sarah as she and Faith peeled the potatoes and carrots and chopped the cabbage in the kitchen at the back of the cottage. 'I thank the Lord daily that you work for such good, kind people.'

The six members of the Holman family had a jolly meal in their small parlour brightened up on this festive occasion by bunches of holly and mistletoe gathered from the Commons and a picture of Mary, Joseph and the baby Jesus in the stable under a bright star chalked by Naomi on her slate and propped proudly on the mantel shelf. During the afternoon Faith sat in her old favourite place on the linen chest in the window looking round at her family. Her father and brother were sitting at the table enjoying a game of cribbage, Rebekah was working at a tapestry and Naomi was sitting on a stool at her mother's feet, holding a skein of wool for Sarah to wind into a ball ready for knitting. Everyone was smiling and relaxed, having enjoyed a good meal, and Faith wondered what the future held in store for them all.

One morning in the New Year Peter Holman appeared in the kitchen of North Hill House seeking his daughter. Beads of sweat stood out on his brow, despite the cold morning, from his hurried climb up the hill and he was in a state of great agitation. Faith happened to be alone in the kitchen and she was humming a tune to herself as she put cups and plates on a tray for the family's breakfast. She looked up, surprised at her father's voice, thinking it was Joseph she could hear coming in through the pantry. 'Whatever is the matter, Father?' she asked, sitting him down at the table and pouring him a mug of ale.

'It's your mother,' he gasped, still short of breath, 'can you come and see her?'

'Is she ill?'

'Not physically, I think, but she seems mentally afflicted. I don't understand why. I don't know what to do with her. I need your help.'

Faith was touched by his distress and said she would go and see her mother as soon as she could get away. She wondered, however, what she would be able to do that her father or sisters could not. Peter finished his ale and wiped his sleeve over his face as he got to his feet. 'I must away to the mill. You'm a good maid,' and he gave his daughter a quick hug before taking his leave. Faith's heart went out to him. Such a kindly, uncomplicated man and it could not be easy living with the volatile Sarah.

After she had cleared away the breakfast dishes, Faith begged Cook to spare her for an hour or so which she did, reluctantly and with much tongue-clucking. Faith wrapped her cloak around her, glad of its deep hood against the biting air, and slipped her feet into her pattens to keep her out of the worst of the mud. As she went down the hill she could see men working in the fields. One was ploughing, patiently pacing back and forth behind his horse, carving out a furrow with flocks of gulls wheeling, raucous, overhead.

At the dark little house in Mill Street Faith kicked off her pattens on the door-sill and went inside where she found Sarah kneeling at her prie-dieu, sobbing. Faith flung her cloak over a chair and went across to her mother, laying a hand on her shoulder.

'Whatever ails thee, Mother?' she asked, shocked at the older woman's evident distress. 'Come, calm yourself, this won't do you any good.'

It took Faith some time to persuade her mother to get up off her knees and sit with her on the chest in the window through which a shaft of weak winter sunlight penetrated and warmed them a little. Faith took hold of one of her mother's hands to offer her some comfort. Physical contact was rare between them but Sarah seemed glad of it. At last she began to speak:

'Yesterday in church the Reverend Powell announced that Archbishop Laud is dead. What has the country come to when the head of the church is executed? Now the Puritans will have their way. Oh, Faith, everything is changing and it frightens me! What will become of us all? People are not obedient to authority any longer. Who'd have imagined people would rise up against their King? The country is torn by war and you don't know who your enemies are. Why, even Mistress Tucker next door complained about a Royalist soldier who is billeted on her and, when I said, "Better a Royalist than a Roundhead", do you know what she said to me?' Faith shook her head as her mother turned anguished eyes towards her. 'She said, "I'd rather have a Roundhead if he was quiet and polite and not always drunk and farting, as my lodger is"!'

Faith had difficulty controlling a sudden urge to laugh at her mother's indignation and most uncharacteristic language.

'How can she excuse the rebels?' Sarah continued. 'What sort of men defy their King?' She shook her head in disbelief.

Faith thought briefly of Robert and said, as gently as she could, 'Some men see things differently, Mother. They feel the King is not being fair to his people - - -'.

'But he is the King by Divine Right! What right has any man to go against him?' Sarah took a deep, shuddering breath to calm herself. 'Anyway, we must be guided by our betters in these matters and no-one is more strongly for the King than the de Beres.'

'Well - - -'. Faith felt it wisest to say no more at this moment. As a young person she did not share her mother's fear of the old order changing. She could not understand her grief at the death of a churchman they had never seen far away in London. Although she realised she must appear loyal to the de Beres for the sake of her job, she felt she was entitled to her own opinions and not obliged slavishly to follow theirs if she felt them to be wrong, even if she was only a kitchen maid.

Faith stayed with her mother until she had calmed down and was almost her normal self again. Sarah patted her hand and said, gruffly, 'Thank 'ee for coming, maid. You'd best be off back to your master's house, and I have gloves to sew, but have a taste of broth before you go.' Faith sipped a ladleful of her mother's rich broth which was simmering over the fire and then she put on her cloak once again and took her leave. As she walked through Taddiport and laboured up North Hill, slipping on the cold, muddy ground in her unwieldy pattens, she wondered about her mother and her melancholy, troubled nature.

During the following months, Sarah Holman appeared to have come through her emotional crisis and, whatever might be going on inside her head, she appeared outwardly calm.

In the country at large events were changing the course of history. Serving at supper one day, Faith heard General de Bere talking of the New Model Army that had been formed by Parliament. It was a disciplined fighting machine to be feared and the General had heard about its leaders. 'Cromwell is a Puritan with a mission. They say he prays a lot. But,' he conceded, 'he's a good soldier. So is Fairfax. Their New Model Army will make mincemeat of our disorganised rabble. Why, even our commanders cannot stop quarrelling amongst themselves.'

Mention of the name Fairfax made Faith think of Robert and she wondered where he was and what he was doing now.

Robert had joined the New Model Army. He had realised his ambition to fight under Fairfax and his respect for that man grew daily. In battle Fairfax was wild and fearless, leading from the front which earned him the nickname 'Fiery Tom'. However, he was also a fair and caring man: fair in his dealings with a vanquished enemy and caring towards his men. To him they were not merely a fighting machine but individuals for whom he always had time for a personal word and an ear for what they had to say.

Robert felt guilty when he thought of home. He had not stayed there long, feeling restless, unable to settle down, and had set off once again to join the army. So far, things had gone well for him. Despite taking part in some hot skirmishes, he had remained uninjured and he was fit and healthy, able to endure the hardships of battle. He was a sociable man and enjoyed the company of the other soldiers during cheerful evenings in taverns or taking part in friendly bouts of wrestling and cudgel-play. Cock-fighting and bull-baiting were forbidden in the Parliamentary army but this was no loss to Robert who had no time for cruel sports.

Every moonless night the troops went poaching to supplement their monotonous diet and one evening Robert was crouching, watchful, in some heather when he heard the voices of two men talking nearby. No rabbits would appear with them making that noise, he thought irritably, and then he noticed that one of the men spoke with the soft vowels and rolled Rs of the West Country and he found himself smiling in the darkness as he was reminded of Faith. He thought of her saying his name and a tug of longing caught at his heart. He wondered how she was and whether he would ever see her again.

TWELVE

Faith perched on the gate looking out towards the sea and breathing in the fresh early morning air. The sky was a cloudless blue but the horizon was hazy. A perfect day for May Fair. The first swifts of summer scythed overhead uttering their piercing shrieks as they swooped in and out under the eaves of the house where they were repairing last year's nest. Feeling light of heart, Faith jumped down from the gate and skipped across the yard to the pantry door.

Cook was in the kitchen stirring the contents of a large pot over the fire. 'Her ladyship wants a hot drink and Jane is indisposed this morning – really, there's always something the matter with that girl! – so you'll have to take it up to her. It's all ready over there on the table.'

Faith picked up the tray, on which Cook had set a pewter goblet and jug of warm buttered ale, and climbed up the back stairs to her mistress's bedchamber on the floor above. Elizabeth de Bere sat up in her four poster bed propped against a bolster and a heap of lace-edged pillows. Her night-gown and cap were white as were her pillows and sheets and the inner curtains and valance of her bed while the outer curtains were of rich red velvet which matched those hanging at the deep mullioned windows. An elaborately carved chest of cypress wood to repel the moths stood at the foot of the bed. Faith knew it contained her mistress's underwear perfumed with muslin lavender bags.

'Good morning, my lady', she curtsied at the door and then stepped across the floor, taking care not to slip on the highly-polished wood with her tray. She set the goblet down on the bedside table alongside the heavy brass candlestick, which she herself had shined with vigorous polishing the day before, and poured her mistress a generous measure of ale.

Elizabeth de Bere stretched and yawned with the languor of an overfed cat. 'Draw back the curtains for me, Faith. Then you can get my clothes ready. I shall wear the pink gown at the right hand end of my hanging closet.' She kept Faith running back and forth, helping her wash and dress, fetching her things, and then, just as the girl was about to go, she asked, 'Will you help me with my hair? That Jane is become quite heavy-handed.' Faith fixed her mistress's fair hair in a neat bun with a ribbon to match her gown and her curls arranged around her face to her satisfaction. Able to escape at last, she had her hand on the handle of the door when Elizabeth de Bere, who was delving in her jewellery box, called to her: 'Oh Faith! Be so good as to take care of the girls today. My husband and son are out on militia business and I have decided to spend the day with my sister. She wishes me to join her in some water-colour painting and the girls would just be in the way.'

Faith's heart began to race with foreboding but she

managed to ask calmly enough, 'Where is their tutor, my lady?'

'He is gone to Barnstaple to purchase some books and won't be back till late, though I don't see what concern that is of yours.' Lady de Bere frowned with irritation at her request not being immediately granted.

Faith persevered. 'As you know, my lady, my sister, Naomi, is to be May Queen today and I dearly wish to see her crowned in the town square. I would gladly take with me the mistresses Susannah and Eleanor who would enjoy the procession and the dancing, I'm sure.' Faith stood quite still, holding her breath, covertly crossing her fingers behind her skirt.

Elizabeth de Bere shook her head impatiently, 'Oh, I had quite forgot it was May Fair. What a nuisance! I don't wish my daughters to mix with the hoi polloi.'

' 'Twill only be the townsfolk and people in from the country, my lady.' Faith tried not to show her annoyance.

'Exactly! Who knows what germs they might catch or what improper language they might overhear? No, I cannot permit it.' Elizabeth de Bere shut the lid of her jewellery box with a snap as though the matter were settled but, with Faith, she should have known better. Faith was particularly determined on this matter and, after all, Lady de Bere had granted her permission to go when she had asked a few days previously.

'My mother has made Naomi a special dress, she is so thrilled with it and so excited at being May Queen, she would never forgive me if I didn't go and see her.' Her mistress's face was stony. Desperately, Faith made a final suggestion. 'Perhaps Master Miles would entertain his sisters while I go and see Naomi crowned?'

Lady de Bere snorted derisively. 'I think not! My

younger son has far better things to do with his time than mind his sisters. Anyway, he is gone to Barnstaple with his tutor. Come now, no more pleading, the matter is settled.' She picked up her hairbrush and started to titivate the row of little curls which fringed her face and pointedly ignored Faith.

Shaking with anger at her mistress's lack of sympathy, at her going back on her word and at her casual dismissal of an event which meant a lot to Faith and her family and, indeed, to all the local people, Faith left the bed-chamber. She said no more, not trusting herself to speak civilly any further.

Down in the kitchen she crashed the tray down angrily on the table causing the jug and goblet to perform a jerky dance.

'What ails thee, maid?' demanded Cook, rolling out pastry.

' 'Tis the unfairness of things!' burst out Faith. 'It's as if I count for nothing.'

'Well, none of us do in the overall plan of things.' Cook nodded sagely, hanging a great sheet of pastry from her rolling pin and then laying it expertly over a huge apple pie. 'We're here to serve our betters, they serve the King and he is answerable only to God. That's the way it is.'

'Aren't we allowed any say in things for ourselves?' asked Faith, rebelliously, as she wiped the tray and flung it on its shelf.

'Rarely. And the sooner you learn that the better,' Cook rejoined, trimming and crimping the edge of her pastry.

Faith ran around doing her chores – sweeping the hall, peeling vegetables, feeding the hens – and then ran up to her room to change into her best grey dress. By the time Susannah and Eleanor came to look for her, after their mother had departed for Great

Potheridge, her mind was made up.

'What shall we do? What shall we do?' asked little Eleanor, clasping Faith's hand and jumping up and down.

'I don't want to stay indoors doing needlework or reading, it's too nice and sunny,' declared Susannah. Unwittingly, she had given Faith her cue.

'Let's walk over to the town. It's a special day and children of your age will be dressed up and dancing. It'll be great fun, I promise you.'

Susannah looked rather put out at being classed as a child with Eleanor but, for once, she said nothing and her younger sister skipped about in glee, holding up her skirts and kicking her heels.

'Come on then!' Faith laughed at the child's uninhibited enthusiasm and they set off along the drive and down the road towards Torrington. They could already hear the jangle of church bells over in the town calling people to the May Fair celebrations.

Over the river they climbed up the long hill nearly to the castle ruins and turned in to the left towards the noise and bustle of the town square. There they were met by a heaving throng and Faith caught hold of Eleanor's hand.

'Now, mind you stay close to me, both of you. I shall be in terrible trouble with your mama if I go home without you.' I probably shall be, anyway, she thought but decided to worry about that later and to enjoy the present.

They worked their way through the press of people round in front of the Black Horse where, even at that hour of the morning, men swayed in the doorway and leant against the windows, bleary-eyed and spitting in the dust. Hastily, Faith led the girls further up the square and managed to find a spot in front of Symonds's greengrocer shop where they could squeeze through and see what was going on. People made way, albeit somewhat grudgingly, for the two smartly-dressed little girls. Eleanor stood on tiptoe and was fascinated by everything she saw, especially the children of her own age who were lining the route the procession would come, dressed in their best clothes and clutching posies of flowers.

'Why haven't I any flowers?' she looked up at Faith out of enquiring blue eyes.

'I didn't think of it, little mistress. We could have picked you a posy on the Commons.'

Just then the young people of the town came dancing into the square. They had been performing the floral dance around the town and were all bright-eyed and breathless. Faith saw Rebekah in a group of four as they circled round and stepped back, then on again. She was wearing a pretty dress she had made for herself especially for this day and was partnered by Will Avery who was looking hot and sweaty in his Sunday jacket.

There was a bit of a commotion behind Faith and Tom Symonds appeared carrying a wooden apple box. He thumped it down on the ground, upturned. 'For the little maid to see better,' he smiled, half bowing before pushing his way back to his shop.

'Nice man!' declared Eleanor, lifting her skirts and climbing onto the box. 'You may share it now and then,' she said looking down rather haughtily at her sister. Susannah was trying to maintain an air of disdain and disinterest about the whole proceedings but she did hop up every so often, nevertheless, to get a closer look at what was going on.

The floral dance had finished and the dancers had dispersed into the crowd. A handbell clanged and a strident voice cried, 'Oyez! Oyez! Oyez! All good people of Great Torrington please stay silent for the proclamation to be read. God save the King!' It was the Town Crier in his black jacket with a red and gold-edged collar, red waistcoat and black top hat with a gold band around it.

Then the town Clerk stepped forward in his wig and black gown. 'The right worshipful the Mayor of this town doth give you all notice that there is a free fair to be kept this day within the town of Great Torrington - - -.' When he had read the proclamation, he led the Mayor, Roger Moune, and honoured guests in a procession to seats on a raised wooden dais next to the Town Hall from where they could watch the proceedings in comfort.

Suddenly, the blare of a trumpet rent the air and the crowd fell silent. Then a murmur rose at the bottom end of the square and everyone stood on tiptoe, straining to see. The musicians, who had accompanied the floral dancers on recorders, lutes, viols, shawms and tambourines, gathered in a group by the dais and struck up a measured rendition of 'Early One Morning.' Eleanor turned to Faith, her eyes sparkling, and said, 'Your song!'

'Here come the Heralds!' declared a woman nearby and everyone jostled for a good view. Faith put a hand on a shoulder of each of the girls to steady them in the crush.

Two boys leading the procession passed in front of Faith and her charges with heads held high with pride, feet stepping in time to the music. They were dressed in blue breeches, hose and long fitted jackets with lace at the collar and cuffs. On their heads were large-brimmed hats with dashing plumes, their shoes had shiny silver buckles and swords hung at their sides.

Faith caught her breath when she saw Naomi following behind the Heralds. She looked enchanting in the white dress her mother had made for her and carrying a posy of primroses, forget-me-nots and lily of the valley. Her dress was yoked in lace, tight at the waist with a sash of pale blue. It had puffed sleeves and a full skirt. Her fair hair hung loose and shining down her back and her face was flushed with excitement as she beamed at everyone. Her bearing, as she paced up the square, was a disarming combination of regality and childish joy.

There were murmurs of appreciation and approval from the crowd and Faith was filled with pride as she leaned towards the girls perched on their apple box and said, 'That's my sister, Naomi!'

'Your sister?' Eleanor turned to face Faith, nearly losing her balance. She had not thought of Faith having a life and family outside North Hill House. 'She's beautiful!'

'How old is she?' asked Susannah.

'Eleven, the same as you.'

'It must be wonderful to have everyone looking at you and admiring you,' said Susannah, and then, somewhat begrudgingly, 'she looks lovely.'

Naomi was followed by six Attendants, younger girls of about seven years of age, all dressed in matching pale blue dresses and straw bonnets and carrying small baskets of primroses. Behind them came another older girl carrying a crown made of plaited flowers and leaves. She, too, wore a long white dress and her hair loose.

The boy Heralds escorted the Queen to her red velvet 'throne' under the splayed ribbons of the maypole at the top end of the square, and the Attendants to their positions alongside, and a great cheer went up as the Crowner lifted up the floral crown and placed it on the May Queen's head. Naomi sat smiling and radiant. The two de Bere girls were entranced. Susannah had abandoned her air of superior indifference and watched the scene before her with wide-eyed interest.

The musicians struck up a fresh tune and the children, already holding their ribbons, performed the slow and stately 'Spider's Web' dance. There were two maypoles, one at each end of the square topped with bunches of yellow gorse traditionally gathered on the Commons that morning by the schoolmaster. As the Queen and her entourage were presented by the Heralds to the Mayor, whose wife gave them silver lockets and bracelets and coins to the boys, the dancers skipped the lively 'Plait' and 'Barber's Pole'. Faith tapped her foot in time to the familiar melodies, remembering how she had taken part in these dances as a child, and Eleanor clapped her hands in delight at the patterns made by the ribbons.

Finally, the Queen led the procession back down the square followed by the maypole dancers skipping in pairs and the local dignatories at a rather more stately pace. When they had all disappeared around the corner by the Black Horse, the onlookers were free to move and the square was filed with a milling, chattering, laughing crowd.

Faith bought some suckets which she shared with the girls. They were savouring these candied fruits as they made their way out to the Commons when they met Rebekah with Will. Faith told them this was her other sister and they gave her sugary smiles and curious glances as Rebekah dropped them each a curtsey. As they walked back down the Commons paths they were full of the day's events, plying Faith with questions: how was a girl chosen to be May Queen or Crowner, or an Attendant, or a boy to be Herald? Who made the costumes? Who was the man in the top hat with the bell and the loud voice? And the man in the red robe edged with fur and the heavy gold chain round his neck? Why did the maypole ribbons not get tangled? They were interested in Faith's sisters and Rebekah's young man and asked Faith whether she, too, had a young man. Eleanor, with the directness and innocence of childhood, suggested a match with Wreford or Stephen. Faith managed light-hearted, non-committal replies on this last subject.

 She had wondered whether to ask the girls not to tell their mother where they had been but they were so full of the day's events it would have been unreasonable to have expected them not to say anything, especially Eleanor. Lady de Bere would see they had come to no harm and Faith hoped their enthusiasm and obvious enjoyment might win her round. Unfortunately, such hopes were to be short-lived.

THIRTEEN

➤❦➤

'Mistress wants to see 'ee straight away in the drawing room,' announced Cook, bustling into the kitchen from the hall door, rolling up her sleeves. 'I told 'ee not to take the maids up to May Fair but you wouldn't listen.'

Faith looked at her from the fireplace where she was stirring an enormous mutton stew for supper in a large black pot suspended over the flames, her face flushed from the heat. She bit her lip and said nothing, just wondered why Cook had to look so pleased about it all.

She ran out into the yard and splashed her face quickly under the pump, drying it hurriedly on her apron which she then tried to flap dry and smooth down. As she returned to the kitchen she tucked escaping tendrils of her thick, heavy hair in under the edges of her little cotton coif. Holding her shoulders straight, determined not to appear cowed, she marched through the kitchen, glared at the broad, plump back of Cook who had taken her place by the stew pot and stepped out into the hall. Her soft shoes were silent on the stone flagged floor as she crossed to the drawing room. Taking a deep breath, she knocked firmly on the heavy wooden door and, as her mistress bade her enter, she walked in, her head held high and her gaze steady though her heart was beating a tattoo inside her chest.

Lady de Bere was sitting bolt upright in her chair, her face clouded by a furious frown, her hands clasped in her lap.

'How dare you disobey my orders!' she burst out, without preamble. 'Exposing my daughters to injury and disease when I'd expressly asked you not to. What do you have to say for yourself?'

Faith stood before her mistress, forcing herself to look her straight in the eye.

'I am sorry you are displeased, my lady, but I made sure they came to no harm. They loved the May Fair procession and were interested in everything that was going on around them. I think it was good for them to be amongst ordinary folk.' Straight away she realised this last statement was a mistake.

'It is for me and my husband to decide what is good for our children, not a serving girl!' snapped Lady de Bere. 'Susannah is quite overwrought from the pressing crowds and Eleanor is far too young to know what activities are suitable for her.'

'I'm sorry, my lady, but I did so want to see my sister as May Queen and you had said I could. She looked so pretty and happy, I expect your daughters told you about her?' Faith's attempts to win her mistress round failed dismally. Lady de Bere waved her hand, dismissively.

'I have not the slightest interest in your family's activities. My concern is for the well-being of my children and the fact that you, who are in my employ, saw fit to disobey me.' Her plump face was beginning to look quite comical, with its flushed cheeks and blazing eyes, but there was no cause for mirth in her next words: 'You will forfeit this week's wages and be confined to your room until Monday and then, perhaps, you will have learnt your lesson.'

Faith stared, horrified, at her mistress. 'But - - - .'

'Don't argue with me, girl, just be thankful I haven't dismissed you. Now go! I don't wish to see you before Monday.' Deliberately, she turned away from Faith and, picking up her needle, bent towards her tapestry which was stretched on its frame beside her and peered at it with great concentration.

Faith was quaking with anger as she left the room but was sufficiently in control of herself to close the door quietly behind her so as not to show her feelings. Out in the hall she stood for a moment looking about her at the grand staircase with its elaborately carved balusters, the family portraits gazing solemnly down upon her and the chandelier with its forest of candles. She had thought this place so fine and grand but now, all of a sudden, it had become abhorrent to her. She could not stand it a moment longer. She ran up the main staircase to the landing above and from there up the back stairs to her attic room where she frantically began gathering up her few possessions and flinging them on her bed. She tied them up in her shawl, looked round her bare room and crossed to the window high in the wall to have one last look out over the countryside.

As she crossed the bare floorboards to the door, Faith realised what she was doing and, dropping her bundle on the floor, she sank down onto her bed. What would her parents say if she turned up on the doorstep of their cramped cottage – for where else would she go? – with no job, seemingly in disgrace.

Her mother, especially, would be distraught for she was always telling Faith how fortunate she was to work in comfortable surroundings for such good employers. She would have to share a bedroom with her sisters once more, when they had got used to the extra space, and she would have to find work at the glove factory or in the woollen mill. Taking a deep, juddering breath, she reached for her bundle to untie it and, when her few clothes were hung up once again in the corner behind the curtain and her hairbrush placed beside the washing bowl and jug, she lay back on her hard bed meekly to await her fate.

She must have dozed off for she awoke with a start to the sound of hammering outside her door, a sound too loud and continuous to be someone knocking to come in. 'Who is it?' she called, but there was no reply. She got up off her bed and walked over to the door but, when she tried to lift the latch, it would not budge. She rattled it furiously but to no avail. Then she heard footsteps walking away along the landing and down the stairs. She was suddenly frightened by her imprisonment and by the eerie silence of her gaoler.

Few sounds of activity filtered up to Faith's room at the top of the house. She heard the sound of horses' hooves and men's voices round in the stable yard. She heard the clank of the pump as water was fetched and Cook's yell to Joseph ordering him to get a move on. Poor old Joseph! He would be running around for the next few days while Faith was in detention.

For someone used to being busy every minute of the day, the enforced idleness was hard to endure. Faith walked about her room, stood on tiptoe and peered out of her window, lay on her bed and tried to think of how many songs she knew. She was softly humming one of her favourites when she heard slow footsteps approach, a scuffling at her door followed by a hesitant tap. She fell silent and stayed where she was, watching the door slowly open.

Joseph's grizzled head appeared and he peered round at her before coming in carrying a plate of bread, a mug and a pail of water. ' 'Twas all I was allowed to bring 'ee, maid,' he said, shamefaced, as he thrust the dry bread at her and dipped the mug into the pail of water, tipping the rest into her washing pitcher. He did not offer any comment about her situation but, before he turned to go, reached inside a pocket of his jerkin and pulled out a folded sheet of paper which he handed to her with no more than a grunt. She opened it up and found it to be a note from Stephen.

'Dear Faith,' he had written in his bold, curling hand. 'Please forgive me for being away to Barnstaple yesterday. I had quite forgot it was May Fair and that you wanted to see your sister crowned Queen. Of course, I would have occupied the young ladies had I been here. Please accept my sincere apologies for having let you down in this way.

'I hope your few days in confinement will not be too unbearable and I will endeavour to make them less so.

'My lord thinks the punishment out of proportion to the crime but my lady insists upon it and reminds him that management of the maid-servants is her concern. She will calm down shortly, I am sure.

'Affectionately yours,
Stephen'

Faith was grateful he had written and pictured him seated in the library, or perhaps in the privacy of his small room on the floor below, bent over the letter, dipping his quill pen into his inkwell and scratching it across the surface of the paper. She pondered over the 'affectionately yours' and lay back on her bed imagining what it might be like to be intimate with Stephen. It was with such thoughts in her mind that she fell asleep, his letter still clasped between her fingers.

The next morning Faith leapt eagerly out of bed after a deep, refreshing sleep. As always, she crossed barefoot on the wooden floor to look out of her window to see what kind of day it was. The sky was clear and blue and the sunlight caught the treetops in its early rays. Humming quietly to herself, Faith poured water into her washing bowl and splashed her face and neck and under her arms. Once dressed and her hair brushed and plaited into a thick rope down her back, she tipped the water into her chamber pot and carried it to the door to take it downstairs and out beyond the stables and laundry where there was a pit dug amongst the trees especially for this purpose. It was only when she came to lift the latch and was unable to, it being secured on the other side, that she remembered her predicament.

It hit her hard, cruelly deflating her joy and energy on this bright summer's morning. In a moment of fury and defiance, she crossed to her small window, pushed it wide and flung the contents of her chamber pot out through the opening shouting, as she did so, 'Gardy loo!' as they did in the towns. She waited, growing suddenly fearful, for an indignant shout from below but none came. Breathing fast and giggling weakly with relief, she sank back down onto her bed to wait.

When Joseph brought her bread and water for breakfast, he lifted up his jerkin and revealed beneath it a length of thin rope coiled and tied around his waist. He unfastened it and stowed it under Faith's bed. 'Master Metherell got it from your brother and he said to tell you to hang it out of your window once it gets dimpsey. When you hear an owl hoot, haul it back in.' Revelling in the intrigue of his message, Joseph nodded conspiratorially as he straightened his old leather jerkin, his rheumy eyes sparkling.

As it grew dark, after a seemingly endless day, Faith gently let the rope out of her window, having first tied the end to the leg of her bed. She gazed out at the evening sky and saw a nail-paring of a new moon appear above the trees with an attendant bright star. The air was mellow and fragrant after a warm day.

Later, an owl called from the woods, or perhaps nearer at hand, and, remembering, Faith hauled steadily on the rope feeling a weight on the other end. Eventually, a basket appeared and Faith manoeuvred it carefully over her narrow windowsill. Inside, wrapped in muslin, she found a wedge of cold chicken pie, a hunk of fruit cake, a piece of cheese and an apple. Underneath she found a small book which turned out to be a volume of poems by a writer called John Donne. She leafed through it to start with, unaccustomed to reading poetry, and then studied individual poems in detail, savouring the sound of the words and trying to work out their meaning. Saturday and Sunday passed far more bearably with a food parcel to look forward to and something to read. She enjoyed Donne's poems and memorised some of them which particularly took her fancy:

'I wonder by my troth, what thou, and I
Did, till we lov'd? were we not wean'd till then?'
Others she set to music in her mind:
'Goe, and catche a falling starre,
Get with child a mandrake roote.'

Faith's imprisonment came to an abrupt end on the Sunday night. It was over as suddenly as it had begun. Lady de Bere's maid, Jane, came to Faith's room in a state of great agitation. Usually, she behaved in a rather superior manner towards Faith, mindful of her situation as a lady's maid compared to Faith's more lowly position as kitchen maid. This evening she stood in the doorway wringing her hands, looking resentfully at Faith who was reclining on her bed reading poetry.

'My lady says you are to come at once and help her with her hair. She is trying a new style and blames me for it not going right. She is getting more bad-tempered by the minute, so hurry, do!'

FOURTEEN

❦

'Yes! Yes! Yes! cried Sylvia Moune in wild abandon as she clasped Wreford's thrusting body closely to her. He, in turn, uttered moans of release and collapsed upon her, burying his face in her abundant auburn hair. When his breathing had quietened to normal, he rolled over and they lay side by side on their bed of ferns.

'What a wild girl you are under that demure exterior, Mistress Silvery Moune!' he chuckled, using his pet name for her. ' 'Tis just as well 'tis dark and away from things in this corner of the Commons, or we would have people coming to see what we were up to!'

Sylvia laughed, the thought of their having an audience giving her an extra frisson, and nuzzled up to Wreford, catching his earlobe between her teeth and giving it a sharp nip. He yelped and turned towards her but a pain in his loins, which was growing more persistent of late, made him feel quite nauseous for a moment and unable to renew his attentions to Sylvia as she clearly wished him to.

'This ground is damnably cold and hard tonight!' he declared, to cover his feeling of inadequacy. 'Let's repair to an inn to warm ourselves up.'

The darkness hid Sylvia's pout of disappointment from him. She knew it was useless to argue or try and cajole Wreford into further embraces once he had had enough so, sighing quietly to herself, she retrieved her undergarments and straightened her dress and hair as she scrambled to her feet. She refused to take his proffered hand as they picked their way up the sheep tracks through the ferns towards the town.

'You're not looking well this morning, son,' General de Bere addressed Wreford at breakfast. 'Is it on account of imbibing too much in the ale houses?'

'I think not, Father.' Wreford's heavy-lidded, blood-shot eyes, underscored with dark marks, avoided the General's gaze. ' 'Tis rather a slight fever I seem to have contracted, I know not how. No doubt 'twill pass in a day or so.'

As he washed down brown bread with a gulp of ale and wiped his mouth and whiskers with a damask serviette, his father continued to look at him thoughtfully but said no more. His mother, meanwhile, declared Wreford to look 'dreadful poorly' and urged him to return to his bed where she would personally administer cold poultices and soothing drinks.

'I'll be fine, Mother, please don't fuss!' Wreford replied curtly and, turning to his father, enquired, 'Is it true that the Prince of Wales is coming to Devon?'

'Yes, indeed. He and his advisers have moved their headquarters from Bristol, where there is the threat of plague, to Barnstaple.'

'Oh, my lord!' Elizabeth de Bere was in a flutter of

excitement. 'Is there any chance he might come to visit us here at North Hill? You are, after all, a most loyal subject and in charge of a sizeable militia. Think of the honour such a visit would confer upon us and, I must confess, I am curious to see what the young Prince is like.'

The general smiled at his wife's enthusiasm and at the wide-eyed excitement of his two young daughters who had been following the conversation while eating their bread and milk. Even the generally sardonic Miles appeared interested at the thought of a royal visitor and his tutor looked expectantly at the General, awaiting his reply.

'It is not beyond the realms of possibility, my dear, but I dare say he has more pressing business to attend to than socialising with local gentry.'

'Such as trying to unite the commanders of his father's forces,' said Wreford. 'We need a strong western army if we are to stand up against the New Model Army and help the King regain his kingdom.'

'Yes, the squabbling in the Royalist ranks is doing the King's cause no good at all,' agreed his father. 'Mind, I feel sorry for Sir Richard Grenville. It seems he has been replaced before Plymouth by Sir John Berkeley and was promised, in exchange, an appointment as Lieutenant General of the Prince's army. However, that position has gone instead to Lord Goring so Grenville is most displeased. I believe he is trying to reorganise the forces he once commanded but he no longer has any authority to act. 'Tis a shame for a strong leader of men to be cast aside in such a manner.'

'Perhaps he has displeased the King in some way?' Stephen spoke up for the first time, not altogether sure he was wise to do so. He had heard rumours that Grenville had been feathering his own nest by collecting money but using it for non-military purposes. But General de Bere would hear no word spoken against Grenville stoutly defending his record as a strict disciplinarian who kept his men under tight control unlike some of the other Royalist commanders who allowed their men to indulge in all manner of excesses: plundering, taking free billeting and coercing the civilian population.

'The Prince needs to take such matters in hand otherwise the people here in the West will no longer support the King and will welcome the rebels with open arms.'

Lady de Bere shook her head in dismay causing her blond curls to bob around her face. 'People are so fickle! How can they go against their King?'

In July 1645 the young Prince of Wales accepted the de Beres' invitation to visit them. He was on his way from Barnstaple to South Devon and, together with members of his Council who were travelling with him, stayed for two nights at North Hill House. The servants were thrown into a flurry of activity readying quarters for the royal visitor and his men and preparing quantities of food. Lady de Bere was frantically trying to decide which of her dresses were most suitable for receiving a prince.

A banquet was planned for the first evening of the Prince's visit, to which local gentry loyal to the King were invited, and General de Bere asked Stephen and Faith to provide some music after the meal. In between preparing food for the visitors and helping with dusting and making beds, Faith managed to find time to meet Stephen in the library to decide upon and rehearse a programme.

'I never thought I would have the honour of playing before a future king. Are you not a trifle overawed, Faith?' he asked, as he stacked the sheets of music they had selected into a neat pile on top of the harpsichord.

'Yes, I am. I shall just have to pretend he is a local gentleman of limited importance so as not to be too nervous. I am interested to see how much the young Prince resembles the portrait of his father in the salon, whether he has the same thin pale face and melancholy eyes.'

Faith was to discover that Prince Charles was nothing like his father in appearance. Although still only fifteen years of age, he was tall and broad-shouldered and rather gypsy-like with his dark skin and mass of black curly hair. His features were coarser than his father's – a big solid nose, heavy chin and full lips – and there was nothing melancholy about his friendly smile and loud laugh and his hooded, sensual eyes. Faith could see that already he was fond of a good time and she imagined that when he became king he would have plenty of music and drinking and women and laughter at his court. He watched her with interest as she sang and when, afterwards, she curtsied before him he caught hold of her hand and raised it to his lips.

'Beautiful music from a beautiful lady,' he declared, admiration showing in his dark eyes. Then, turning to include Stephen, 'Thank you, too, Master Metherell. You play excellently well. You make a very handsome couple,' he added, laughing at their blushes.

The following morning the Prince held a meeting in the library with his Council and General de Bere and other local Royalist gentry to discuss the situation in the West. Lord Goring's forces had encountered the Parliamentary army under Fairfax near Langport in

Somerset and had been decisively defeated. Goring retreated with more than six thousand horse and foot soldiers to Bridgwater and from there to North Devon. He advised the King's secretary, Lord Digby, to collect into a single army all the Royalist forces in garrisons or trained bands throughout Devon and Cornwall, and those before Plymouth, to confront the strong New Model Army which was marching westward. Otherwise, Goring felt the entire West would be lost. The Royal Council quickly agreed to this plan and renewed efforts were made to raise a sufficient Royalist force to face the Parliamentary army.

'I am on my way down to the South Hams and thence to Cornwall,' the Prince said to General de Bere. 'Grenville is to come with me. Will you accompany me also? I'd welcome a man of your experience.'

'I should be honoured, Your Highness,' General de Bere said, without hesitation, bowing his head before the young Prince.

Elizabeth de Bere had very mixed feelings about her husband's departure. She was proud that the Prince had requested his company but fretful at the thought of being without him at North Hill House, especially in such troubled times. Wreford was furious and disappointed at being left behind, even though his father was entrusting him with the running of North Hill House and putting him in charge of his militia. He would much rather have been riding with the Prince and hoping to see some action.

'The young Prince requires the support of men who have experience of warfare,' said General de Bere, 'and, anyway, son, you need to get yourself well.'

Wreford proved to be a tyrannical ruler of North Hill House. His advancing illness affected his reason and his moods, making him unpredictable, and the servants crept about their business trying to keep out of his way. His mother seemed unable or unwilling to control him.

Lord Goring established his infantry at Torrington, after having called in additional forces from the surrounding hundreds, and they were camped on the outskirts of the town. At the same time, the major body of Goring's horse was allowed to take free quarter in the region between Barnstaple, South Molton and Torrington and, by their behaviour, made themselves very unpopular. The lack of discipline and inactivity of his men, together with a declining confidence in the Royalist cause, brought about a rapid reduction in Goring's forces during the summer of 1645.

Wreford heard that Goring enjoyed a few drinks and jokes and a game of cards and quite frequently invited him and his men to North Hill House where they would carouse all evening and into the early hours. Faith hated these sessions as she was expected to wait up to be on call to serve the men drink and refreshment. She loathed having to go into the dining room where they sat around the table in varying degrees of drunkenness, leering at her and reaching out to paw at her as she renewed their supply of ale and wine.

One night she was sitting in Cook's chair by the kitchen fire nodding off to sleep. Lady de Bere had long since retired to her bed-chamber and Faith had taken up her hot milk. Even Cook had gone to bed. Only old Joseph continued to sit on his stool, leaning forward, elbows on knees, puffing his clay pipe and gazing into the glowing embers of the fire.

Suddenly, the door from the dining room crashed open and Wreford staggered into the kitchen on legs he appeared to have no control over. Faith would have laughed at the sight of him if he had not also looked alarmingly threatening as he lurched towards her and grabbed hold of the back of her chair. She scrambled hastily to her feet.

'More ale!' he bellowed, his bloodshot eyes staring, his colour high. 'More ale needed in there for my friends.'

'Pardon me, young master,' croaked Joseph, 'but do you not think you should retire to bed now? It's been a long night and you look mortal tired.'

'Who are you to tell me what to do, old fool?' Wreford took an unsteady step towards Joseph and aimed a swipe at his head but missed and nearly lost his balance. Drunk and confused he paused then, looking blearily at Faith, said, 'Perhaps bed isn't such a bad idea, especially with attractive company. Help me upstairs, Faith.'

Faith recoiled in distaste and fear but Wreford clutched her arm in a powerful grip. She looked at Joseph in an appeal for help but he had risen from his stool and was slipping out through the pantry door. Although she knew he would be unable to do much to help her, she was shocked at his speedy escape. She was left alone to cope with this terrifying situation. She tried to shake her arm free from Wreford's grasp but he merely held her more tightly and clutched her body to his in a feverish embrace. She nearly choked on the fumes of drink and some underlying rottenness that he breathed over her and twisted her head away from him. 'Let go of me, please!' she begged, struggling, and then, as he persisted in crushing her to him, she pummelled him with her fists and shrieked, 'Let me go!'

Anger and panic were fighting for control of her when she heard footsteps and Amos burst in through the pantry door with Joseph puffing and panting behind him. His face was dark with fury as he grabbed hold of Wreford and wrenched him away from his sister. Wreford turned towards him, belligerent, and raised an angry fist. Amos did not hesitate and felled him with a single blow to the jaw.

As their master lay sprawled on the stone floor, Faith flung her arms around Amos's neck in a hug of relief and gratitude. Then she drew back, suddenly anxious for her brother. 'I hope this won't cost you your job,' she said, but he merely shrugged and she thought she detected a strange gleam of triumph in his eyes.

'Don't you worry. 'Ee won't remember a thing in the mornin',' Joseph reassured them.

'Thank you, Joseph, for fetching Amos.' Faith looked gratefully at the old man who had shuffled over to the fireplace and sunk down onto his stool once more.

'Didn't want you suffering the same fate as your ma,' he muttered, his face expressionless as he fumbled for tobacco in the pocket of his jerkin.

Faith looked enquiringly at Amos who shook his head and looked perplexed. 'What d'you mean, Joseph?' she asked.

'P'raps I didn't ought to say, maid.' He hesitated and stuffed coarse shreds of tobacco into the bowl of his pipe with gnarled fingers while Faith and Amos stared at him, ignoring the semi-conscious Wreford spread-eagled at their feet. ' 'Tis said your mother's first son 'tweren't your father's. 'Twas the General's.'

Faith and Amos stood motionless, stunned, trying to absorb this incredible information. Then, before either of them said anything, Wreford began to stir and groan. Amos stooped and, grabbing hold of him, hauled him to his feet. Putting Wreford's arm around his shoulders and supporting his buckling body, he said, 'I'll get 'ee up to his bed,' and half dragged, half carried his master over to the door.

FIFTEEN

The New Model Army proved to be the most effective military instrument of the entire Civil War. It was a national body, well-disciplined and regularly paid to carry out Parliament's wishes. Sir Thomas Fairfax was the Commander of this army, Philip Skippon its Major General of Foot and Oliver Cromwell the Lieutenant General of Horse.

By early 1645 this army was in the West Country, having taken the city of Bristol. Most of England was now under Parliamentary control and Fairfax had been instructed to consider the state of the West and, particularly, the safety of Plymouth.

After the fall of Bristol, the Royalist commander, Lord Goring, was told to push through enemy lines to join the King who, together with Montrose's forces in Scotland, would then be in a better position to strike a last blow at London. Goring, however, had no intention of leaving Devon. He stayed in Exeter and his army remained in the county in the same state of 'negligence and disorder' as before. Goring's behaviour became increasingly erratic and in November he took off to France for two months supposedly to 'recover his health'. He had maintained a sizeable force in Devon for five months, causing the local people much grief and hardship, and yet had done nothing constructive for the advancement of the Royalist cause.

The Prince's Council finally decided to collect what troops they could in Devon and Cornwall, place them under the personal command of the Prince of Wales, and march east in order to relieve Exeter and drive the Parliamentarians out of Devon. In December the Prince and his followers, including General de Bere, crossed the River Tamar and settled his court at Tavistock. Preparations proceeded satisfactorily into the new year when news was received of a general advance of Fairfax's army. The Prince then retreated into Cornwall leaving Wentworth's horse to protect the border. Lord Hopton was appointed as Lieutenant General to reconstruct an army to face the New Model.

Despite the success of his army, Fairfax knew that the task facing him in the West Country was no mean one. He and his men must contend with a large force of experienced horse and a considerable body of Cornish foot, many of whom had been put in strongly fortified garrisons throughout Devon. Exeter, Barnstaple, Dartmouth and Torrington had been heavily reinforced and care taken to strengthen forts at Tiverton, Salcombe, Exmouth and Ilfracombe as well as forces being established at a number of country houses. However, Fairfax was well-informed about the disunity and dissension within the Royalist ranks and aware of the weakness of local forces which were poorly disciplined and rarely paid. It was no secret that the Cavaliers were hard put to raise money and supplies. They plundered the countryside and paid nothing for what they took, whether it be free lodging, farm produce or horses. Devonshire people had had enough of the looting of Royalist troopers. They refused aid if they could and would do anything to rid the county of Goring's horse.

By the autumn of 1645 the advance of the New Model Army was welcomed with relief by the majority of Devonians who were sick of war and desired to return to law and order and the protection of property and did not care which side dominated as long as peace prevailed. The fact that theirs was a losing cause did not help the Royalist leaders in gathering recruits and in keeping their soldiers from deserting.

Faith's mind was troubled as she plodded down the road from North Hill House making for the market in Torrington, a basket over her arm. It was a day of sunshine and sudden brief showers and fleeting rainbows. The trees on Pollard's Hill had taken on a wonderful variety of hues – orange, green, brown, yellow, red – giving an overall russet effect. The River Torridge, full after recent rains, was a rich muddy brown as it rushed high between its enclosing banks and Faith caught sight of the bright blue-green and orange flash of a kingfisher as it flew low over the water.

The news of William, her mother's first child, being General de Bere's had come as a great shock to Faith. Maybe it was just a rumour. She could see how her mother's pious manner might lay her open to such malicious gossip and perhaps she should forget the whole thing. Then she remembered butcher Huxtable's drunken remarks outside the Black Horse after church and wondered how widely known the rumour was.

At the door of her parents' cottage she hesitated and thought about how she could broach the subject with her mother. Sarah was not the easiest person to talk to about personal matters.

Inside the cottage, Faith found her mother sitting in her usual place by the hearth, her hands (a little swollen around the joints these days) guiding her needle deftly in and out of the seams around the fingers of a glove. She greeted her eldest daughter in her unemotional, matter of fact way and, before Faith could decide how best to ask her about William, said, 'Have you heard that the Mayor has met his Maker?'

'Roger Moune, dead?'

'Yes, killed, they say, in a violent encounter on the Commons last night.'

'Who would do such a thing? Did he have enemies? I thought he was a popular Mayor.'

'I understand it is somehow connected with his daughter who has been foolish.' Sarah's expression was a mixture of sadness and disapproval. 'Talk of a baby or an illness. Rumour connects her with Master Wreford but one is not wise to listen to rumour.' Sarah broke off her thread with a firm bite of her still strong teeth.

'It is true they have been walking out, I've seen them together,' said Faith. 'Is it thought that Master Wreford killed the Mayor?'

'Well, so it is whispered, I do believe. Him, or one of his men. I can't believe it of the young master.'

'He has been acting wild and strange of late. I think he is not a well man. He looks out of feverish eyes and his moods swing violently. I try to keep out of his way.' Faith did not elaborate upon Wreford's behaviour, not wishing to worry her mother about her own safety at North Hill House.

She wanted to ask about William. She was not

usually reticent about speaking what was on her mind but her tongue suddenly became a large, dry, cumbersome thing which filled her mouth and she simply could not bring herself to ask about the paternity of Sarah's first child. 'Where is Father working today?' she asked instead. She always found him so much easier to talk to than her mother.

'He's carting baize up to the rack park. He'll be up there now. He came by a short while ago and popped his head round the door on his way past.'

'I'll maybe call by and see him.' Faith took up her basket. 'I'd best be off.'

'God go with you, child.' Sarah remained in her seat as Faith swiftly crossed the swept earth floor and kissed her lightly on her forehead.

'And you, Mother.'

Faith started up the steep street. There were a number of Royalist soldiers strolling about or lounging in the doorways of their billets. They looked with interest at Faith and greeted her with a 'Good day to you, pretty maid', or started whistling a ditty as she walked past. Faith merely nodded and smiled.

Before reaching the top of Mill Street, she made an abrupt left turn up some steep, narrow steps between two cottages which brought her out into a sloping meadow. Here, amongst the crowded racks perched on the side of the hill to catch the prevailing westerly wind, she found her father.

He did not see her at first, busy with his work, lost in his own thoughts. When she called to him, he looked up and smiled his slow smile as she approached.

'Good to see you, daughter!' He planted a rough kiss on her cheek. 'How is it up at the house with the General gone?'

'Master Wreford is becoming ever more unreasonable and the place is swarming with soldiers who treat it as their own, ordering food and drink as though there were endless supplies. In the evenings the men get drunk and the master has to be helped to bed. My lady appears not to notice and spends her time shut away in the drawing room or her bed-chamber, or visiting her sister at Great Potheridge.'

'Well, see you take good care of yourself, maid.'

'Yes, I will, Father.' Faith took a deep breath and decided to speak of what was on her mind. 'Father, there is something I would like to know. I've heard a rumour that my brother William was not your son,' she hardly dared to look at him, 'but General de Bere's. Can this be true?'

Peter Holman did not appear shocked or angry, merely saddened and resigned as though he had known this moment would come one day. He looked into his daughter's enquiring eyes and said, 'Aye, 'tis true, maid.'

'I thought the General was different from his son,' said Faith. 'I've always found him a rather distant, upright sort of gentleman.'

'She told me 'twas only the once. The General was in his cups and she a young maid unable to prevent his advances. She was near mad with worry when she found she was with child and wanted to break off our engagement.'

'But you didn't let her?' Faith stood stock-still, her hands clutching the handle of her basket as though grasping on to life itself, her eyes riveted on her father's face.

'No. I'd always loved her. I loved her still and she needed my help so we married and, when the boy was born, I called him my own.'

'So, how did people know?'

'Gossip spreads in a small town like Torrington and

people remember such things. I'm sorry you had to hear it from another.' Peter's face became clouded for a moment. ' 'Twas after she had William that your mother took to religion, out of remorse, she was never so religious before.'

'Remorse? What about General de Bere? Did he feel no remorse for taking advantage of a servant girl?'

'The gentry are not held accountable for their actions,' Peter smiled ruefully. ' 'Tis the way of things.'

Faith felt her eyes smarting with tears of sympathy for her humiliated mother, her good, kind, faithful father and anger at the unthinking arrogance of her master and his family and all those like them.

Peter gave her a quick, clumsy hug and then pushed her away from him gently, saying, 'Be off with you, Faith, and do your shopping and I must get all this baize racked before I can go for my dinner.'

She took a path along the side of the hill that brought her out at Windy Cross and made her purchases at the bustling market down in the square. She passed the time of day with people she knew but was not inclined to chat. Her mind was too full of her own thoughts.

She returned to Taddiport by way of the Commons instead of going back down Mill Street. It was quieter here amongst the brown ferns which smelt sweetly after the last shower. Folk were working on their strip fields at the bottom of the hillside across the river. All the rest of the land on the hill belonged to the de Beres.

Up beyond Taddiport Faith stopped outside the Huguenot's cottage. The door was open and she heard unusual sounds coming from within: scrapings, crackings and crashes. As she hesitated, the weaver appeared, clearly distraught, his hair standing on end, his face stricken. In his arms he held what looked like a bundle of sticks which he dumped down in a heap outside his door. He turned to go inside again, not having seen Faith.

'Is something the matter, Master Bosanquet?' she enquired, perturbed by his appearance.

He looked up, startled to see her standing there, and, when he spoke, it was in French, such was his distress: 'C'est mon métier à tisser détruit! Mes moyens d'existence perdus! On l'a brisé en morceaux!'

'I beg your pardon?'

He looked at her in a dazed manner and ran his fingers distractedly through his dishevelled hair. 'It's my loom, my livelihood, destroyed! They've smashed it to pieces!'

SIXTEEN

Robert pulled on his new woollen stockings and stout leather boots, recently supplied to all the men in the New Model Army, and wriggled his toes in delight. God, it was good to have dry feet at last! He had been tramping around this damp county of Devon for months and felt he had been knee-deep in mud for ever. It was now cold as well. At least he had a horse to make life easier. Some of the footsoldiers had been in a bad way, their boots so far gone they had been marching with straw-stuffed rags tied around their feet. It had been a hard time and Robert was thankful that he was fit and strong.

After taking Tiverton in October 1645, heavy rains had impeded the Parliamentary army's efforts to besiege Exeter and they rested instead at Crediton where Oliver Cromwell and his cavalry joined the main body of the army. Robert was surprised, the first time he saw Cromwell, at how plain-featured and shabbily dressed he was but to hear him speak was an inspiration. The man had charisma, a powerful and persuasive tongue and seemed to be lit from within by his religious conviction. Robert only had to listen to him speaking for a few moments to understand why men were prepared to leave their homes and families and work to follow him. When he had occasion to talk to him personally one day, with a message from Fairfax, Robert was almost overwhelmed by the directness and intensity of his gaze and felt that Cromwell could see right into his very soul. The rest of the army were given a boost of confidence by the presence of Cromwell and his 'Ironsides'.

Fairfax managed to secure the blockade of Exeter establishing garrisons at key points around the town. The remainder of the army were withdrawn to Ottery St Mary to take up winter quarters. Fairfax was concerned with the well-being of his men, many of whom were dying from exposure as a result of the wet winter weather, a lack of good clothing, adequate supplies and sufficient quarters, and it was mainly for this reason that the Parliamentary army remained inactive during November.

Encouraged by reports of the weakness of the Parliamentary army, the Royalist forces were regrouping at Tavistock and Okehampton for an attack which they hoped would secure Devon once again for the King. But nothing came of their efforts and by the end of November the leading Royalists were in winter quarters at Truro.

In early December Fairfax decided to move westward in response to renewed enemy activity and in the hope of finding improved surroundings for his sick men. Robert was in one of the advance units sent across the River Exe to take possession of Crediton and fortify it while the remainder of the forces left Ottery for Tiverton where Fairfax established his headquarters for the following month. During the next two weeks he tightened his grip around Exeter by gradually taking control of the great houses and thereby cutting off supplies which were coming through from the South Hams. Having established these outposts, the Parliamentarians consistently harassed the Royalist garrison, going right up to the walls of Exeter.

Just before Christmas the Royalist army was massing at Okehampton to make a concerted effort to relieve Exeter with great stores of provisions. The Parliamentarians decided on an immediate rendezvous and show of force and this was enough to deter the make-shift and ill-prepared army the Prince of Wales had intended to lead. Reports of Parliamentary troops gathering at Cadbury Hill between Crediton and Tiverton, together with cold and snowy conditions, persuaded the Royalists to keep to their quarters and the New Model Army returned to their camps.

In the New Year of 1646 the Royalists were recruiting men and collecting supplies as best they could. The Prince and his advisers were at Totnes but their attempts to urge the army to march on Exeter for its relief did not work. Many men refused to come into the army and many deserted.

The New Model Army, equipped with new shoes and stockings, began its advance westward on 8th January. The bulk of the army made for the South Hams. One contingent marched to Okehampton to mislead the enemy and engaged some Royalists at Bow. Cromwell led a body of horse and foot towards Bovey Tracey and, entering the village after dark, took the enemy completely by surprise, catching some of the officers playing cards. Many of the Royalists escaped into the night but four hundred horse were captured.

On 10th January the New Model Army arrived at Ashburton, finding it recently abandoned by the

Royalists, and the same at Totnes and nearby South Devon villages. The Royalist opposition was collapsing completely in panic and defeat. On 13th January Plymouth was freed after three years of continuous siege and on 18th January Dartmouth was captured, destroying Royalist hopes of aid from France. The Royalists were forced to retreat into Cornwall.

The bulk of the New Model Army returned to Exeter to continue the siege and to Barnstaple to attack the stronghold there as well as Royalist cavalry still in the county. At the end of January Fairfax received word of the westward penetration of some of the King's horse from Oxford and of Royalist horse in North Devon attempting to push eastward to join them. He decided, once again, to postpone an attack on Exeter and to leave it securely blocked up while the army marched westward.

It was only on 8th February that the Parliamentarians learnt of the extent of the danger confronting them, that a general massing of Royalist forces was taking place under Lord Hopton. Word had it that the Royalist intention was to relieve Exeter and join with the Oxford horse in an attempt to recapture the West. Barnstaple was to be the base of operations and, with North Devon securely in Royalist hands, they could hope to bring in additional aid from Wales or Ireland. Fairfax, therefore, decided to advance in person with a force of some 9,500 horse and foot hoping this time to completely destroy the Royalist armies.

On 14th February Robert set off with the New Model Army from Crediton, where they left their baggage and heavy equipment, for Chulmleigh on the road to Torrington which Hopton had fortified four days before. Wet weather hindered their progress once again and it was 16th February when they got to

Ashreigney where a general rendezvous was held. General Cook was sent, meanwhile, to Barnstaple with a sufficient party to blockade that town and prevent reinforcements from getting through to Hopton's aid.

As they marched on towards Torrington, Robert found himself thinking about Faith caught up in this war. He wondered if she still remembered him after nearly a year and a half. Perhaps she was married by now? This thought caused him a curious stab of pain though he knew he had no right to feel that way. Was she fiercely on the side of the Royalists, like her employers, or was she, like so many ordinary people in Devon, just anxious for peace and for life to get back to normal, not caring which side won? He flattered himself that, after speaking with him, she might have some sympathy for the Parliamentary cause.

Robert had seen many people welcome Fairfax and his army with open arms as he freed them from the burden of the constant plundering and free quarter of Royalist forces. Fairfax was always fair and compassionate in the terms he made with captured Royalists and soldiers who had formerly fought for Royalist militia came over to the Parliamentary side in droves.

Robert gave his horse a friendly pat on the neck after he had successfully negotiated a deep ford without getting his master too wet. He had a different horse now to when he last came to Torrington, a sturdy grey with dark mane and tail whom he had named Prancer as he was more lively than his previous horse. He owed his life to his old faithful chestnut, Trooper, who had been killed at Naseby, shot from under him in the heat of battle. The horse's flanks had protected Robert who had lain beneath him, feigning death, and later been able to escape suffering no more than a few cuts and bruises. He wondered whether his luck would hold in the forthcoming battle.

~~~

There was a feeling of unease at North Hill House. Drums and bugles mustering the soldiers had been sounding on and off all day over in Torrington and everyone was saying a battle was brewing.

Faith continued with her usual chores in the kitchen. Thoughts of recent events and revelations chased each other around inside her head: the relationship between General de Bere and her mother when she herself was a serving girl at North Hill House; the possible implication of Wreford in the murder of the Mayor and what had happened to his daughter, Sylvia, who seemed to have disappeared; Master Bosanquet and his wrecked loom. Her father thought Huxtable and some drunken friends might be behind the destruction. It seemed that Bosanquet had refused to do some weaving for Huxtable's daughter, that, having shown her how to do it, he had insisted that she finish it for herself and she had made a mess of it. Huxtable was mad because, in his eyes, she had been made to look a fool by the 'Frenchie'. He resented the fact that Bosanquet had taught his daughter in the first place. Bosanquet could not afford another loom and Peter managed to find him a job for the time being in the woollen mill – only doing fairly menial tasks – but the Huguenot was grateful for his help.

In the evening there was a stamping and snorting of horses in the yard as Wreford gathered together the North Hill militia. He had received word that an army of rebels was advancing and gathering at Stevenstone House over on the other side of Torrington and that Lord Hopton required every man in the town and its surroundings to support the Royalist cause. Faith threw a shawl around her shoulders and, taking up a lantern, went out into the yard. Every man from her master's estate was there – except for the master himself – either on horseback or on foot, carrying a long pike. Only old Joseph was left behind to keep the home fires burning. Faith moved among the men and horses like a shadow fascinated by the mixture of emotions she could sense: eager expectation, apprehension, bravado, fear. She looked into their faces and exchanged a few words with some of them. Suddenly, she found herself gazing up at Stephen sitting motionless, his face in shadow. 'Take care,' she said to him touching him lightly on the knee and he merely nodded solemnly, resting his hand on hers for a moment. She searched for her brother amongst the crush of men and horses and found him at last, waiting patiently for Wreford's order to set off. 'God go with thee, brother.' She looked up at Amos who smiled his slow, warm smile so like his father's and reached down to clasp her hand for a moment. 'And with thee, sister.'

Just then a scream split the air, startling the men and unsettling the horses, and everyone turned to see Elizabeth de Bere running down the front steps into the yard.

'Wreford! Wreford! Where are you.'

'Here, Mother. What ails thee?'

She pushed her way between the horses to her eldest son and clung desperately onto his leg. 'What is Miles doing amongst you? Answer me that. He's far too young! I forbid him to go!'

Wreford looked down at her, a sneer on his still handsome though haggard face, a strange light in his eyes. 'He's no younger than the Prince of Wales and quite old enough to fight to protect his King and country. Stop whimpering, madam, and get on with your womanly duties and let us men get on with ours!'

He turned his horse away from her and shouted at the men to follow him. Lady de Bere was dumbfounded at her son speaking to her in such a tone and simply stood shivering with shock and cold, watching as the men filed out of the yard and along the driveway. She stayed there until the clatter of hooves and the tramp of their feet on the road down to Taddiport had faded into the night air. Then, bursting into tears, she ran back to the house, calling for her maid, Jane. As she walked round to the pantry door, Faith found it was Robert she was thinking of and she wondered whether he was amongst the soldiers on the opposing side.

~~~

Fairfax and his army drove the Royalists from the Rolle mansion of Stevenstone on the eastern side of Torrington and the soldiers, tired after the day's long march, settled down to rest before the next day's battle. It grew dark early on that winter's night and it became colder but at least the sky had cleared and, for once, it was dry.

Some scouts were sent out in the early evening on a recce towards the town. When they were only half way there they met some Royalist footsoldiers and there was a fierce skirmish across the fields in the gathering darkness. Hopton ordered his men back from the outposts closer to the town.

Fairfax decided simply to strengthen the positions gained and stationed his men in readiness for an attack on the town at dawn. All was quiet over Stevenstone Park and the surrounding fields except for the coming and going of the sentries between the watch-fires and the muttered exchange of the Parliamentary watchword, 'Emanuel, God with us', when patrols met.

Later on in the night the distant sound of a tattoo beating over in the town reached the ears of the Parliamentary soldiers. Fairfax ordered a company of dragoons forward to the barricades to find out if it signalled a retreat and they were met by a volley of fire from Royalist musketeers who were lying in wait for them. Two more companies of dragoons galloped down in support and footsoldiers charged bravely and recklessly after them.

The whole army had been stood to arms in the park. Robert noticed that the moon was rising into view above the trees as he fixed his sprig of furze, which was the agreed signal to show he was on the Parliamentary side, into his steel helmet. Trumpets sounded the signal to mount and, with 'Fiery Tom' at their head, Robert's troop of horse, together with four others, trotted off towards the town accompanied by three regiments of foot, their drums rolling.

The battle raged all along the town's defences where the King's men fought Parliament's men for every hedge. Robert and his fellow soldiers got through eventually to the final barricades, piled tree-trunks across the mouth of Calf Street, but before they could break through someone set light to them and great sheets of flame rose up into the night sky lighting up the faces of the men on both sides. When the barricades had subsided into glowing piles of twigs and ash, the Parliamentary soldiers broke through into the town. There was fierce fighting in the narrow streets, where men struck out with their musket-butts like clubs as they were too close for firing, and the townspeople watched with terrified faces from upper windows.

Hopton's men made a desperate counter charge and Robert was horrified to find himself forced back to the smouldering barricades. Then, just as it seemed that Fairfax was not going to be able to contain the Royalist horse who were trying to drive them back into open country, there came the blast of trumpets as Cromwell appeared with the reserves and the Parliamentary army then swept into the town and took control of the square. An injured Lord Hopton and his Blue Coats were caught up in the retreat and the streets of Torrington were littered with dying men from both sides and abandoned weapons.

———

Amos sat in the church, his back up against one of a group of barrels stored in a corner. He pulled off the white handkerchief, that had been tied around his right arm as a signal that he was on the Royalist side, and dabbed at the blood trickling down his cheek. He was very dispirited. His heart was not in this battle. He had no fervent Royalist feelings, in fact he felt a good deal of sympathy for the Parliamentary cause, as far as he understood it. Perhaps it was his lack of commitment that prevented him from fighting fiercely enough. He hated fighting and in close hand-to-hand combat was slow to strike the first blow. Before he knew what was happening, he had been struck from his horse by a hefty blow to his cheek from a musket-butt. He managed to crawl to the side of the street where he lay semiconscious out of the way of the trampling hooves and boots until he was rounded up with other prisoners and marched into the church. He was wondering whether his cheekbone was broken – it certainly hurt like hell – and was becoming aware of other bruises acquired when he tumbled from his horse onto the cobbles, when a familiar voice nearby said, 'What a mess! I can't see us winning this one. The rebels are too strong for us.' It was the herdsman from North Hill House, Martin Slee.

'I wonder what will become of us?' Amos mused, looking round at the couple of hundred or so men in the church. 'They do say Fairfax is a fair man.'

Martin reached into the pocket of his jacket and pulled out his pipe. 'A bit of baccy will help pass the time,' he grinned, packing the bowl with coarse, flaky tobacco. He looked round for a means of lighting it and finally took up a hymn book from one of the pews and irreverently ripped out a clutch of pages which he rolled up and stuck into a lantern resting on one of the window ledges. After a few coaxing sucks and blows, Martin got his pipe going and, just as the flame was about to burn his fingers, he flung away the twist of paper which fell down amongst the barrels.

Robert had managed to come through the fierce fighting in the town unscathed. He had become separated from the rest of his troop and found himself amongst Cromwell's men as they pursued the last of the fleeing Cornishmen down steep, slippery cobbles to the river. As Prancer's hooves clattered over the bridge at Taddiport, he suddenly had a vivid memory of standing there with Faith and a desperate longing came over him at the thought of her. So engrossed was he with his recollections and emotions that he failed to see a Royalist horseman in the shadows. The flash and crack of a musket shot caught his attention too late and he cried out as a searing pain swept through his left thigh. Somehow he managed to stay on his horse and, grunting with pain, rode on with the other soldiers towards Holsworthy. He cursed himself for letting his mind wander and not being fully alert. Wreford, the man in the shadows, also cursed for not bringing the rebel off his horse.

Suddenly, from back in the direction of the town, there came the roar of a mighty explosion which caused the ground to tremble and echoed around the hills before subsiding in a long-drawn-out rumble. The Parliamentary soldiers reined in their horses and looked at each other in amazement.

'Whatever was that?'

'P'raps 'twas the wrath of God!'

'Sounded like the powder store blowing up.'

'Just look at that glow in the sky!'

Turning, with difficulty, in his saddle, Robert looked back towards the town whose buildings stood out in black silhouette against a sky of deep, livid red. The agonising throbbing in his thigh made him feel sick and rather light-headed and his voice, when he spoke, was little more than a hoarse whisper: 'It's Torrington burning!'

SEVENTEEN

╼❧╾

The morning following the Battle of Torrington found Wreford sitting at the table in the kitchen of North Hill House with his brother, Miles, Stephen and members of his militia. For once he forgot his superior station, such was the feeling of camaraderie amongst the men after the hard fighting of the night before. Cook had provided them with hot, newly-baked bread, large pats of freshly-churned butter and hunks of strong cheese. Faith was to-ing and fro-ing from the pantry with leather-jacks of ale and stone flagons of cider.

'That was a lively encounter last night!' Wreford's eyes flashed feverishly. He poured more ale into his pewter tankard and scratched impatiently at some ugly-looking spots that were showing above his lace collar. He was excited at having been involved in some action at last and was still fired up by the experience even though it was a blow to his pride to have been on the losing side.

'Those Roundheads were too well-organised for us,' said Hugh Mortimore. 'Someone pointed out to me Sir

Thomas Fairfax right in the thick of it. He'd lost his helmet but was still pushing forward shouting encouragement to his men. He was like a man possessed!'

'My Lord Hopton was brave too,' spoke up Miles, who felt he had matured by some five years after the previous night's activities. 'His horse was shot from under him but he kept on fighting. I saw him myself, a great bloody gash in his cheek, swinging his musket like a club at any rebel who came near.'

'Word is he escaped and made off towards Barnstaple,' said Wreford, a note of contempt in his voice, 'and the Cornishmen scampered back into Cornwall.'

'I thought the world had come to an end when the church blew up!' Stephen spoke for the first time. 'Did you know it was used as a powder store, Master Wreford?'

'No, I did not.'

'Do you think the Roundheads knew about it when they herded their prisoners in there?' asked Mortimore.

'I shouldn't be surprised if they set it off on purpose to get rid of a couple of hundred Royalists,' Wreford snarled, reaching for the bread and tearing off a hunk.

'I'd have to disagree with you there, sir,' reasoned Stephen, 'for Roundhead guards were killed as well and a lot of people in the vicinity. In fact, I heard that Fairfax himself narrowly missed death in the square from a web of lead that fell down from a rooftop right next to him.'

'A pity it didn't finish him off and strike a blow to the Parliamentary cause,' growled Wreford.

'What will the King do now?' asked Miles, looking questioningly at his older brother. 'And the Prince of Wales who, with our father, is effectively trapped in Cornwall?'

'I dare say the Prince will make for France. The King has been anxious about his safety for some time now.'

There was a reflective silence amongst the men for a while broken only by the chomping of jaws on bread and cheese, the slurping of ale and the puffing on pipes until Joseph suddenly asked in his cracked old voice, 'Has anyone seen Amos or Martin?' The men looked at one another and tried to remember when they had last seen the groom and the herdsman.

'Hiding out somewhere, I shouldn't be surprised,' sneered Wreford, looking provocatively in Faith's direction. 'I expect they found the battle a trifle hot for their taste, neither being keen fighting men, though Martin's accustomed enough to the spilling of blood in the slaughter house.'

The men looked slightly uncomfortable and avoided Faith's eye as she moved amongst them except for Stephen who caught her hand as she passed by him and gave it a little squeeze of sympathy. She managed to maintain a cool, aloof expression though she was boiling with indignation inside. It was true that her brother was a gentle man who avoided trouble where he could, and he was not so fervently in support of the Royalist cause as some, but he was no coward. He was prepared to do his duty, as he saw it.

Faith left the kitchen on the pretext of fetching a bucket of water from the pump in the yard but really to escape for a few moments from the smoke and battle talk of the men. She shivered in the cold February air but relished its freshness after the kitchen and breathed in great gulps. It was a day of wild gusting wind from the west which roared in the trees making the branches creak. Dark threatening clouds raced across the sky bringing sudden heavy, drenching showers, some of stinging hail.

As she cranked the pump handle, a ring dove

caught her attention as it fluttered overhead uttering its anxious throaty call and she watched it balance precariously on a branch in the thrashing trees. A flash of rusty red then came to her notice and, staring harder, she saw it was the gypsy woman wrapped in a dark cloak, her face and hair hidden by a deep hood and her bright skirt glimpsed only intermittently as she walked. The woman stopped short of the house in the shelter of a bank of rhododendrons and beckoned to Faith. After checking that no-one was in sight, Faith ran over to her and looked enquiringly into the woman's sharp eyes.

'A man down in Taddiport needs help. I've made him as comfortable as I can but I think you should go, Faith, but tell no-one here at the house.'

Amos! Fear clutched at Faith's heart. 'Is he badly hurt?'

'Bad enough. You'd best make haste. I have herbal remedies if you need them.'

'What is your name?' Faith had registered that the woman knew hers and wondered how.

'They call me Zillah.'

'And how can I find you?'

'I'm never far away,' the gypsy replied with an enigmatic smile and, turning on her heel with a swirl of her cloak, strode off along the drive towards the road.

Faith hauled the bucket of water indoors and set it down, slopping, on the pantry floor. She ran into the kitchen where the men were beginning to disperse and, remembering though not understanding Zillah's warning not to tell anyone, she said the first thing that came into her head: 'I have to go down to town. I've just had word my mother's been taken ill. I'll wash the dishes when I return.'

Cook's eyebrows bunched together into a frown but, before she could say a word, Faith was out of the door and running up the back stairs to her room to fetch her cloak, her overshoes and the warm gloves her mother had made her for Christmas out of scraps of leather. She managed to slip out of the house without anyone noticing.

As she hurried down the lane, she looked across at Torrington where wreaths of smoke still rose from the town and were whipped away by the strong westerly wind. The outline of the buildings had changed for roofs were broken and jagged and something was missing: there was no church spire!

Where the road grew steep and slippery, Faith kept a sharp look out peering into every gateway, under every hedge, round every tree. She passed the Huguenot's cottage and walked on down towards the huddle of dwellings at the foot of the hill. She cursed herself for not having asked the gypsy exactly where the injured man was and stood opposite the old leper hospital looking about her with increasing agitation. No-one was stirring in Taddiport as if they were keeping indoors after the terrors of the previous night. Perhaps someone had found him already and taken him in, or helped him to his parents' house in Mill Street? She walked as far as the bridge but saw no-one.

Before going to her parents' cottage, she retraced her steps to the hospice chapel peering once more back the way she had come, making sure, and walked a little way along the road towards Langtree. Suddenly, she caught her breath. Wasn't that a boot she could see jutting out from the gateway to a field just before the trees of Servis Wood? She approached the gateway fearful of what terrible injuries she might find.

The man was half sitting, half lying, leaning against the field gate semiconscious. It took Faith a few seconds to register that it was not the kindly, undistinguished features and tousled brown hair of her brother that she was gazing down upon but the jutting nose, firm lips and tumbled black curls of Robert Armitage.

His lobster-tailed helmet was on the ground beside him but he still wore his breastplate over his jacket. Faith looked to see where he was injured and saw a coloured kerchief had been tied round his left thigh, presumably by Zillah, the colours already distorted by oozing blood. She took hold of his arm and shook him gently.

Robert stirred and opened his eyes which seemed to take a moment to focus on Faith. Then they filled with the warmth of recognition and his lips curved into a smile revealing his strong white teeth. ' 'Tis uncommon good to see ye, lass.' He reached out towards her but winced as his thigh reminded him of its wound.

'What happened to you?'

'I was caught off guard when I came through here last night in pursuit of Hopton's Cornishmen and shot by a man concealed just along the road there.' He added, with a grin, 'I was thinking of you at the time and not paying proper attention, though I can't blame you for my misfortune.'

'Faith blushed slightly. 'Is there a musket ball lodged in your leg?'

'No, no, 'tis only a graze but it has bled a lot and weakened me.'

'Have you lain here all night?'

'No. I am returning from Woodford where I camped last night with Cromwell. I have despatches from him for Sir Thomas Fairfax but I'd just come out into the light from yon wood when a blackness descended on me and I fell from my horse. I don't know how I got here to this gateway.'

'Zillah, the gypsy woman, helped you. She told me you were here.' Faith looked up and down the road. 'I don't see your horse.'

'Oh, he's wandered off, most likely. I lost my old Trooper at Naseby and this one lacks his faithfulness.'

Robert gathered all his strength to get up on his feet, grunting with the effort. Beads of sweat broke out on his brow beneath his tangled hair.

'I must get these papers to Fairfax. Will you help me, lass?' Robert gazed down imploringly at Faith as he supported himself on the field gate, taking the weight off his injured leg.

'Of course, though you'll not be going far on that leg. I'll help you to my parents' house, where my mother will treat it for you, and I can take the despatches to Fairfax, if need be.'

He looked with gratitude at her earnest face and would have liked to have planted a kiss upon it but he did not want to appear too forward or to make a fool of himself by losing his balance and keeling over.

They set off along the road towards the river, the tall, solidly-built man limping badly and leaning heavily on the slender girl, his arm around her shoulders, hers about his waist supporting him as best she could.

They passed no-one in the street on the way to her parents' front door which was firmly shut this time of year against the cold and damp. Faith rapped upon the door and, before she could lift the latch, it was opened by Sarah who looked in astonishment at her daughter and the stranger she was holding on to.

'Faith! Whatever are you doing with a rebel soldier?'

'He needs help, Mother, he's wounded. Please let us in.' Faith made a move to get Robert across the threshold but Sarah barred her way.

'No rebel enters this house! We are loyal to the King here.' Her eyes blazed in her thin, worn face. Faith realised, with a stab of disappointment, that her mother was not going to be persuaded. Her own clear green eyes flashed with anger.

'He's just a man, Mother, an injured man whether he be Roundhead or Royalist and he needs help. Where is your Christian charity now?'

EIGHTEEN

Faith barely managed to control a sob as she turned away from her parents' doorway and wondered where on earth she could take Robert to rest and recover from his wounds. He was leaning against the cob wall of the cottage, barely conscious, trying to keep the weight off his bad leg. However, luck was with Faith that day for, just at that moment, Maurice Bosanquet appeared on his way down from the town and, seeing her struggling to support an injured soldier and clearly in distress, he stopped: 'Can I be of service to you, mademoiselle?' he enquired.

'Oh, if you please. I have here a wounded man who needs shelter and help.'

'Then you must come to my house,' said the Huguenot, without hesitation. 'I will support him on this side.'

Robert was largely silent. It was taking all his concentration to keep from stumbling and passing out from the pain of his thigh. It was easier now with another person to help support him – he had not liked to lean too heavily on Faith's slight frame – and they retraced their steps through Taddiport, watched by the odd gaping passer-by, and made their way slowly up the hill to the Huguenot's cottage.

'This is very good of you, Master Bosanquet,' said Faith as he opened his front door. 'I'm afraid my mother was somewhat less than welcoming!'

They helped Robert through into the parlour where the jagged remains of Bosanquet's loom leaned drunkenly in the corner. They sat him in a chair by the hearth while Bosanquet stoked up the fire under a hanging pot of water and disappeared upstairs to fetch a straw mattress. When he had dragged it down into the parlour and they had made Robert as comfortable as possible on it, Bosanquet fetched some clean rags while Faith eased off Robert's boots. A warm, rich, cheesy smell rose from his stockinged feet.

'Sorry, lass,' he grimaced. 'Not much chance of washing when you're on the march.'

She smiled. 'I'm going to have to take your breeches off to get at the wound, otherwise I must cut them and 'twould be a shame.'

'Aye, they're the only pair I have. I hope you'll not see anything that offends you once they're off.' His eyes twinkled in his face that was creased with pain.

'I have a brother. I don't expect you have anything that he has not.' She gave him a mischievous look.

He chuckled, 'I don't suppose so.'

He unbuckled his belt and she helped him ease his breeches down, trying not to catch his wound but the blood had congealed and stuck to the material. 'Just tug 'em, lass, 'tis the easiest way.'

Faith hesitated, unwilling to cause him more hurt than was necessary. 'Could I have a damp cloth, Master Bosanquet?' she asked. He squeezed out a strip of material in the pan of water heating over the fire and brought it to her. Dabbing gently, she was able to unstick the blood and free the breeches from the wound. She gasped on seeing the gash in Robert's leg where flesh and muscle had been gouged away by the passage of the musket ball.

'Oh, you poor thing!' she cried, looking up at his tired, worn face. 'You must be in agony!' She laid her hand for a moment against his cheek in an instinctive gesture of comfort and his dark eyes glowed as he looked at her.

'Could've been worse,' his voice was gruff. 'At least I've still got me leg!'

The Huguenot watched as Faith bathed the wound with the clean rags and bowl of hot water he brought to her. Then she folded a piece of the material into a wad and packed it onto the wound to try and staunch the bleeding and bound a long strip of material round his thigh to hold it in place.

'It needs a poultice to prevent infection,' she said, 'but I have no knowledge of what to use. The gypsy woman said she would help but I don't know where to find her.'

'Zillah will be by presently, no doubt,' Monsieur Bosanquet nodded.

'You know her?' Faith was intrigued.

'A little.' The Huguenot would not be drawn.

'I must get Cromwell's despatches to Fairfax,' said Robert, suddenly. 'I've delayed too long already.'

'You'll not be going anywhere for the time being,' pronounced Bosanquet. 'You must stay where you are.'

'I'll take them,' Faith volunteered. 'I've heard he has his headquarters at the Black Horse. I'd be interested to meet the great Sir Thomas Fairfax.'

Faith set off across the River Torridge once again and up to the town clutching the sheaf of sealed papers that Robert had entrusted to her. She went by way of the Commons rather than Mill Street wishing to avoid any chance of meeting her mother, so incensed was she by that woman's lack of kindness and support. With the wind at her back she strode up through the sea of ferns and grasses. Brown, horned slugs slimed across the muddy paths and shy little hedge sparrows darted about amongst the gorse bushes.

She came upon Zillah who appeared to be gathering berries of some sort. 'How is your Roundhead friend?' she enquired, as Faith drew near.

'He has a nasty deep wound where a musket ball ripped through his thigh. Do you know what could be put on it to prevent infection?'

Zillah nodded thoughtfully. 'I will prepare a poultice and take it to the Huguenot's.'

'Thank you. You're very kind.' Faith smiled into the woman's brown, lined face, fascinated by the piercing flecked eyes, then, remembering her mission, bade her farewell and continued up the hill.

As she came into the town, Faith could hardly believe what she saw. Buildings had holes in their roofs, or no roof at all. Slates were smashed and scattered about, littering the streets, and thatch was burnt. Windows were gaping holes with jagged edges of broken glass. Everywhere there was chaos and destruction.

She made her way to the Black Horse which had survived last night's explosion undamaged save for some broken windows. A Roundhead guard posted at the door directed her upstairs to the chamber that

Fairfax was occupying. She knocked on the heavy wooden door and, as a deep voice within bade her enter, found herself overawed all of a sudden. She could not back out now, however, so she lifted the latch and, heart pounding, entered the room where the Lord General of the Parliamentary army was sitting at a table by the window.

Faith saw a tall, dark, gaunt man dressed in a scarlet uniform coat bent over the despatches he was writing. He had a forbidding appearance to a young girl such as Faith: swarthy skin, unruly black hair hanging about his face and neck, beetling brows and a beak of a nose. As he looked up, with a swift movement of his head, she saw an angry scar, acquired at the battle of Marston Moor, which puckered up his cheek and added to the harsh look of him and she almost took a step back in fright. However, she saw that his dark eyes were warm and friendly as he looked at her. His speech was slow with the same accent as Robert and he had a curious stammer which gave him an air of unexpected vulnerability. His manner was courteous as he addressed her. 'What is your name, lass?'

'Faith Holman, my lord.'

'How can I be of service to you, Mistress Holman?'

'I have with me despatches from Lieutenant General Cromwell at Woodford over towards Holsworthy. They were entrusted to Master Armitage but he was shot and wounded and unable to get here.'

'Robert Armitage hurt? That's bad news indeed.'

Faith was surprised and impressed that the Lord General should know an individual soldier. 'He is in good hands, my lord, and we will do our best to restore him to health.'

'I thank you on his behalf, lass. Is it your family

who have taken him in?'

'I'm afraid not, my lord.' Faith coloured up with shame. 'My mother supports the King and would not have him in the house. My employers are Royalists also, so he is with a friend of mine, a Huguenot weaver.'

'Are you a Royalist, too, or do you have some sympathy for our Parliamentary cause?' Fairfax looked with kind interest at Faith.

'I know nought of politics, sir. I merely wish we could all live together in peace.'

'Amen to that. I thank you for bringing the despatches from Lieutenant General Cromwell. I am at present writing a report to the Honourable William Lenthal, Speaker of the House of Commons, and Cromwell's comments will be most useful. Perhaps you would convey my good wishes to Robert Armitage.'

'Indeed I will, my lord.' Faith dropped a quick curtsey and smiled farewell. She would always remember her meeting with this man – so imposing but kindly – for he had made a strong impression on her.

As she walked down Mill Street the wintry sun was setting and draining the colour out of the land. All the drama was in the sky where banks of clouds were rearing up before the setting sun showing tantalising glimpses of their gold and silver linings against a clear pale blue sky. Overhead a new moon turned its slim, curved back to the sun.

As she passed her parents' house, her father appeared in the doorway and called to her.

'I'm sorry, Father, I'm in a hurry. I have just had an interview with Sir Thomas Fairfax. I had despatches from Cromwell to deliver on behalf of Robert, the wounded Roundhead soldier my mother refused to help. I have to get back to North Hill House for Cook will be in a rage already.'

Peter listened patiently and then said quietly, 'Faith, will you just spare a moment? I have some very sad news to tell you. I'd rather you heard it inside than out in the street.'

Bewildered and apprehensive, she followed him into the cottage. There was no sign of her mother or sisters in the dark little parlour. As he turned towards her, she realised there were tears in her father's eyes and her heart began to hammer in her chest as he said to her, gently, 'It's your brother, Amos. I'm afraid he was killed in the explosion in the church!'

NINETEEN

❦

Faith looked, aghast, at her father wondering if she had heard him aright and then, as a great sob ripped out of her throat, she flung herself into his arms. They stood for some moments comforting each other, quietly shedding tears.

'Why Amos?' cried Faith, at last, stepping back from her father who wiped his sleeve roughly across his eyes and nose. 'He never did anyone any harm. Why couldn't it have been that monster, Wreford? Nobody would miss him!'

Peter smiled slightly at her vehemence. 'His mother would, no doubt.'

'Where is my mother, and my sisters?' Faith asked, suddenly.

'Upstairs. Your mother has taken to her bed.' With a tired, resigned air, Peter walked over to the hearth and threw another log, from the box kept alongside, onto the fire. Faith ran over to the stairs in the corner of the room and, feeling her way in the darkness from memory, climbed up to her parents' bed-chamber where she found Rebekah and Naomi sitting by their mother holding her hands.

'Mother, I'm so sorry!' she managed to blurt out, her former anger at Sarah's refusal to help Robert forgotten for the moment. She was shocked by the pallor and sunken eyes of the face on the white pillow. She briefly hugged each of her sisters who smiled wanly at her as she sat at the end of the bed.

'Now I've lost both my sons.' Sarah's voice was low and wavering. 'It must be a punishment.'

The three sisters could think of little to say that would comfort their mother and they sat in silence lost in their own thoughts and in the hope that simply being together would offer mutual sympathy and support. Faith found herself studying the pattern of squares on the patchwork quilt. Finally, she said she must return to North Hill House and took her leave of her mother and sisters whose brimming eyes were like huge dark pools in the light from the single candle on the bedside table.

She said goodbye to her father, who was sitting downstairs by the fire staring into the flames, and hurried back through Taddiport and began to climb up North Hill. She did not call at the Huguenot's cottage, although she knew she should tell Robert that Cromwell's despatches were safely delivered, for she dared not delay any longer. Also, she felt she wanted, for the moment, to be alone with her grief. She would have to call later with some food, as she could not expect Master Bosanquet to provide everything for Robert, so she could tell him then about her meeting with Fairfax.

As she climbed the steep hill between banks and hedgerows and trees which met overhead in places forming a tunnel, her thoughts were full of her gentle, inoffensive brother who had had the terrible misfortune to get caught up in events. She remembered the tremendous, roaring boom that had rocked the hills and echoed through the valleys the previous night and tortured herself by imagining Amos deafened and blown to pieces by it. She could only hope his end had been swift. The hot tears coursing unchecked down her face cooled rapidly in the cold February air as she toiled up the lane.

***

Later that night, after Maurice Bosanquet had shared his supper of rabbit stew with Robert, they chatted companionably. Robert sat on the mattress propped up by a pillow so he could look around him at the same time as resting his leg which was throbbing badly. Bosanquet sat in his rocking chair gently swaying back and forth.

' 'Tis uncommon good of you to take me in like this when you don't know me from Adam,' said Robert, looking across at the dark chiselled features of the Huguenot.

Bosanquet smiled in his self-contained way. 'Faith has helped me in the past so I am pleased to do the same for her, if I can. She's a good maid. And you seem a reasonable fellow.'

'For a Roundhead!' Robert grinned.

'Poof!' Bosanquet gave a typically Gallic shrug. 'All that is of no concern to me. I am no Royalist.'

'You're not from these parts, I take it. I cannot quite place your accent.'

'I am French. I was a Protestant in a Catholic country. Not a good situation to be in so I came here which was better for me for a time. Then there is this Civil War 'twixt King and Parliament but it does not affect me personally. I continue with my work, people are happy with it, until – .' His eyes strayed over to the jagged pieces of wood in the corner of the room and Robert's followed the direction of his gaze.

'What is that?'

'The remains of my loom. Smashed beyond repair. I have my suspicions of who did it but no proof, so –,' another shrug accompanied by a sigh, 'what can I do?'

Robert sat forward eagerly, forgetting his injury for a moment until it reminded him with a sharp twinge of pain which made him grimace. 'Maybe I could help you when I am a bit more mobile. I'm a carpenter by trade. If you could show me what a loom should look like, and if we could get some wood, I'd gladly have a go at building you a new one.'

Bosanquet looked with gratitude at the eager face of his guest and, fired by the other man's enthusiasm, began to see a spark of hope for the future. 'I could draw you a plan – ,' he began, when there came a soft tapping on the front door. Rather warily, he picked up a candle from the mantelpiece, went over to the door and opened it a crack. 'Ah, Zillah! Come in.' He opened the door wider but she declined his invitation, shaking her head which set her silver earrings clinking and flashing.

'No, thank 'ee kindly. Just take this, 'tis for the young man's wound. Rub it on thrice daily to help it mend and keep this somewhere cool in between times.' She handed Bosanquet a small earthenware bowl covered with a scrap of cloth and, when he looked inside, he saw a mess of herbs mixed into a thick, mushy green paste. When he looked up, Zillah had already turned away and was vanishing down the lane into the night.

'Thank you, madame,' he called after her. 'Good night.'

'Bonne nuit, monsieur,' came the reply, much to his surprise and delight.

The Battle of Torrington signalled the end of the Royalist hopes in the West and this was underlined when, at the beginning of March, the Prince of Wales set sail from England for the Isles of Scilly and thence to France. Life was chaotic and uncertain for many people including those at North Hill House. General de Bere continued to be absent, having accompanied the Prince of Wales to France, and Wreford was becoming increasingly irrational and incapable of running the estate because of his advancing illness. Lady de Bere showed herself to be a person who was unable to cope in a crisis. She relied on her menfolk and, when they let her down, she did not know what to do. More and more she escaped, with her daughters, to her sister's house at Great Potheridge, sometimes staying there for days at a time.

Royalist landowners suffered a great loss of freedom in 1646. Their estates were sequestered, that is, taken over by county committees in London which collected rents and fines and assigned leases. Royalists who were willing to do so might 'compound' for their estates which meant they could buy them back for a fine which was assessed at anything from a half to a tenth of the capitalised value. North Hill House and its land had survived the Civil War intact and the de Beres were determined to retain their property. However, in his confused and enfeebled condition, Wreford refused to make the payments on his fine and, despite warnings that a Parliamentary landlord would take over the estate if the fine remained unpaid, he was unable to grasp this fact and maintained a posture of indignant outrage.

Stephen Metherell's teaching duties were becoming increasingly sporadic and his payment erratic and he confided in Faith that he had applied for a teaching job at King Edward's School in Bath in the neighbouring county of Somerset. She was pleased for him and envied him the opportunity of going to live in a city and of experiencing life in the wide world, although she herself was occupied at present with people and events closer to home.

Whenever she could, Faith slipped out of the house and down the hill with parcels of food for Robert. He was always pleased to see her and she began to realise how much she looked forward to being with him. Her preoccupation with the business of keeping him fed and getting him well had helped her not to brood too much on her brother's death. At the same time, she talked to Robert about Amos and his experience of losing friends and comrades in battle enabled him to understand what she was feeling and to offer her comfort and reassurance. She tended his wound for him, gently rubbing on Zillah's herb mixture and rebinding his thigh. He seemed to get stronger by the day and one morning she found him sitting in Bosanquet's rocking chair by the hearth. The Huguenot was at work at the mill.

'Master Maurice tells me you have a beautiful singing voice,' he said, watching Faith as she unwrapped a piece of pie from a cloth and placed it on a plate. 'Will you sing something for me?' She flushed as she poured a measure of ale from the black-jack she had brought with her and put it on a low table beside him. Then she stepped back a few paces and standing before him, hands lightly clasped in front of her, she sang an old favourite, 'Country Gardens', smiling down at him as she sang.

He sat quietly watching her, leaving his food and drink untouched though he was hungry. He was moved by the freshness of her voice. When she finished, he clapped his hands gently. 'You have a rare talent, lass.' She curtsied playfully.

'Do you know 'The Oak and the Ash'?' he asked her. ' 'Tis a song from the North.'

'I don't believe I do. Can you teach it to me?'

'You'll have to excuse my rough and ready tones, but it goes summat like this.'

His voice had a hoarse edge to it but his sense of tune was true enough and Faith sat before him as he taught her the song: 'A north country maid up to London had strayed – '. By the second verse she was joining in the refrain:

'Oh! the oak and the ash, and the bonny ivy tree,
They flourish at home in my own country'.

She loved the song and they often sang it together in Maurice Bosanquet's parlour, both when they were alone and when the Huguenot was present. Looking at Robert's rugged, friendly face as they sang, his smiling dark eyes, the curve of his lips, the firmness of his chin, Faith thought how familiar and lovable he had become to her and she recognised the feelings that were stirring within her as being a growing desire for him.

One day, when she called by, she found Robert studying a drawing. 'Why, 'tis Master Bosanquet's loom!' she exclaimed, looking over his shoulder.

'I should like to try and build him a new one. He's been very good to me. But I must find out where to get some wood.'

'I'll ask my father, he might know.'

' 'Twould be helpful, lass. And what good things

have you brought for me today?'

'Cold chicken pie, apples and some of Cook's fruit cake.'

' 'Tis a feast indeed! I'm a lucky man,' and he planted a quick kiss on Faith's cheek before limping over to the fireside to sit down.

※

Peter Holman found a supply of wood for them through a woodcutter friend on a local estate where trees were being felled. It was good quality ash and he managed to obtain it at a price the Huguenot could afford. He took a liking to Robert with his openness and lack of pretension. He found him easy to talk to and soon felt he had known him for years. Whenever he had a little spare time he would spend it helping Robert build the loom. It did not take him long to become aware of his daughter's feelings for this man, betrayed by the look in her eyes and by little affectionate gestures she made towards him, and he was happy for her. He sensed that her feelings were reciprocated but he wondered how long Robert intended staying in the locality once the loom was finished. He said nothing, however, for the time being.

Faith called in to North Hill Cottage the very morning Robert had put the finishing touches to the new loom. He was justly pleased and proud of his handiwork and was looking forward to seeing Bosanquet's reaction when he returned from the mill at the end of the day.

'He'll be delighted, I know he will!' Faith, catching Robert's mood of excitement and satisfaction, flung her arms around his neck and hugged him tightly. As she drew back, she felt his arms come round her and looked up into his face as he bent his head towards her and kissed her on the lips. He kissed her tenderly at first and then, sensing her eager response, he kissed her more passionately. He lifted her off her feet and carried her over to his mattress where he gently laid her down. She took off her little white cotton coif and shook her hair free while, very carefully, his fingers clumsy with controlled eagerness, he began to unlace her bodice.

'Will you have to go back to the North now the loom is finished and you are feeling stronger?' Faith asked later as they lay in each other's arms basking in the warm aftermath of love. Robert hesitated, turning away from her for a moment, and then, his brown eyes full of love and regret, he looked directly into hers as he said, 'Yes, I must return. I have a wife. I'm sorry, lass. I should've told thee.'

TWENTY

Faith was perched in her favourite place, on the first rung of the five-barred gate leading from the yard into the field, and looking across the rolling Devon countryside.

She would never forget the utter desolation she had felt on that day when Robert told her he was married. Already deeply saddened by the loss of her brother, Faith had poured all her feelings and needs into caring for the wounded Robert and had grown very fond of him. Just as this fondness had burst into love and she felt open and vulnerable to him, he had shattered her with the news that he had a wife.

She had been stunned for a moment, lying still, staring at him. Then she had sat up and, in a frenzy of despair and disbelief, rained savage blows upon his chest and arms with her clenched fists. Robert had let her continue for a while and then caught hold of her wrists, firmly but gently, and looked with sadness into her face which was distorted in anguish.

'Why didn't you tell me?' she cried, at last.

'I don't know. Cowardice maybe. I didn't want to spoil what we had between us.'

'What's her name?'

'Mary.'

'Have you any children?'

'No.' They were both silent for a few moments trying to control their emotions. Then Robert spoke. 'I've hardly seen her these past three years. I've been away fighting. When I saw her last we were like strangers and I kept thinking of you. I'm so sorry, lass. Can you forgive me?'

Faith shook her head dumbly. She pulled on her linen chemise and, with fumbling hands, hastily pinned up her hair and crammed her coif on top of the roughly-arranged tresses. She scrambled to her feet, hurriedly smoothed down her skirt and laced her bodice and, not looking again at Robert, made for the door of the cottage. She managed somehow to lift the latch and pull open the door and stumble out into the lane. Here, at last, as she started to climb North Hill, the tears came, overflowing from her eyes and gushing down her flushed cheeks. She realised vaguely that she was making an ugly noise, loud wracking sobs and rasping intakes of breath, but she just could not help it and there was no-one to hear except the birds and animals. A greenfinch, perched on a beech twig preening its feathers, looked up startled at her approach and flew up over the hedge with a flash of gold-barred wings and tail.

She had not seen Robert again since that day and did not even know if he was still with the Huguenot. Her father, who had taken to Robert and treated him like a son after the loss of his own, tried to question her gently about what had happened but she refused absolutely to talk about him. Even so, she thought about him constantly, remembering his warmth and humour and passion, wondering if she would experience ever again such a feeling of love and belonging. But it had all been false for he belonged in law to another.

Faith strained her eyes to see if she could catch a glimpse of the sea on the far horizon. She thought she could discern a narrow strip of blue which was a little darker than the sky and wished she could see it close-to and be able to pull off her shoes and stockings and paddle at its edge where it lapped against the land. Robert had described to her the sea as he had seen it on the wild east coast of Yorkshire where the waves thundered in to the shore and in South Devon where it was calmer and warmer to the touch. She wrenched her mind away from him and thought of all the jobs she had to do. Life was even more hectic these days as she now had two masters to run around after.

North Hill House was now officially Roundhead property. As the de Beres had not made any attempt to pay the required fine, the estate had been taken over by Richard Stevens, the second son of a local landowner who had always supported Parliament, together with his wife and three young children. Cook was even more short-tempered these days having to work for a 'rebel' master though he was not an unpleasant man, merely somewhat brusque and impersonal.

Wreford and his mother, brother and sisters had moved into the Lodge House, a modest cottage situated near the main gates of the estate, which formerly belonged to Hugh Mortimore who now lived in Little Torrington. Wreford was gradually losing his grip on reality. His illness was eating away at him, both physically and mentally, and he was increasingly seeking refuge in drink. He rarely got out of his bed these days.

Elizabeth de Bere sustained herself with rage. When she was not at Great Potheridge, she kept to the cottage and railed at the servants, when they came with food or to clean, about the perfidy of Parliament and the unjustness of her situation. Her husband was still absent in France believing his duty to his sovereign to be more important than his responsibility for his family. At the same time as bewailing his abandonment of her, she wished she could join him abroad away from all the humiliation she was suffering at the hands of the rebels.

The haughty manners of Miles and Susannah had been replaced by expressions of hurt bewilderment. Not understanding fully what was happening to his older brother, Miles despised what he saw as Wreford's collapse and loss of will. He went out as often as he could, staying out for hours on end, involved in wild, lawless activities with the sons of other fallen Royalist families. Susannah stayed close to her mother imitating her look of wounded pride and trying, against all the odds, to act the lady of the manor. Only little Eleanor spent nearly as much time as before in North Hill House, going to see her beloved 'Cookie' and playing with the eldest daughter of the new owner who was about her age. She came running out now from the pantry door to find Faith.

'I knew you'd be here. Why do you love this gate so?'

Faith climbed down. ' 'Tis because I can look far away over yon hills to the sea and wonder what it be like there.' Faith smiled down at the child's round, fresh face, cheeks lightly flushed, rosebud mouth slightly open and eyes sparkling with interest.

'Cookie says you're to take some broth to Wreford.' Eleanor took hold of Faith's hand and led her purposefully into the kitchen. Cook wrapped a lidded iron pot in a thick cloth and thrust it towards Faith.

'Now, you hurry back, mind. There's vegetables to be done for the rebel family's dinner.' Cook persisted in referring to them thus, refusing to give them a name.

Old Joseph was sitting by the fire in the kitchen of the Lodge House. He spent most of his time there now, having followed the de Bere family out of a sense of allegiance. However, he was unable to do much more these days than keep the fire going, heat up water, take fresh bottles of wine to Wreford and empty his master's rancid chamber pot. Lady de Bere was irritated almost beyond endurance to find him always sitting there by the hearth puffing his foul-smelling pipe. Jane still attended her mistress and a woman came over from Little Torrington to cook and a young girl to clean but Elizabeth de Bere seemed to expect Cook to continue to provide for them.

Wreford had lost all his power to frighten Faith. She viewed him now with disgust and contempt and the sight of him even provoked a spark of compassion in her. As she entered his evil-smelling bed-chamber with the bowl of broth, she looked at him propped up against his pillows. His hair, once blond and sleek, had fallen out in handfuls making him look as if the rats had been at him. His formerly proud, glittering, pale blue eyes were dulled and bloodshot and his puffy face was encrusted with several weeping sores.

'What is that Roundhead bastard doing to my house?' he rasped, as Faith placed the broth on the table beside his bed. 'I'll dislodge him, you'll see, and be master once again.' Then, not realising the irony of what he was saying, 'What's the use of putting the broth there, girl? I can't eat it from there. You must feed it to me.'

Barely managing to overcome the wave of nausea which rose within her, Faith spread the cloth on Wreford's chest, tucking it in at his collar. She rested the heavy pot on her knees and took off the lid releasing a column of steam and a tasty aroma of chicken and vegetables. She dipped in the spoon Cook had provided and carefully lifted it to Wreford's parched lips. The uncontrolled sucking and dribbling of his mouth and the unfocused beseeching of his eyes as she fed him filled Faith with a curious mixture of horror, triumphant revenge and pity.

The mystery of Roger Moune's death had never been solved. John Voysey, a previous mayor, had taken over his duties. Through kitchen gossip Faith had heard numerous rumours: that Sylvia Moune had been taken to hospital in Barnstaple, pregnant and sick; that her father had challenged Wreford about being the cause of his daughter's condition but had not survived to make his claims public; that the Constable had been to North Hill House asking questions and there had been talk of a trial and the threat of hanging. However, nothing was able to be proved and the case was dropped. If Wreford had been responsible for the Mayor's death, he was suffering retribution enough. He may have escaped the humiliation of a public hanging but he was dying anyway from his illness, a far more painful, protracted death.

Faith felt melancholy as she walked back along the drive to the big house. Ahead of her today and every day for the foreseeable future lay the prospect of a host of household chores. Today, as it was fine, the new mistress had decided she wanted all the bed curtains taken out and shaken and the dust beaten out of the quilts and blankets.

Suddenly, Faith saw Stephen running towards her waving a piece of paper. She smiled to see him, generally so cool and calm, filled with obvious excitement. He was breathing heavily when he reached her. 'You remember I had an interview at King Edward's School last week?' he gasped. 'I've got the job! I start in September after the summer vacation.'

'I'm so pleased for you!' she cried, tucking the empty broth pot under her arm and clasping one of his hands between both of her own. Then something made her add, 'I'll miss you.'

His breathing had quietened to normal and he looked at her earnestly. 'Faith, will you come to Bath with me? Will you marry me?'

Everything around them was quiet as they gazed, speechless, at one another save for a blackbird urgently rummaging around in the undergrowth and a sudden gust of breeze which lifted the leaves of the trees and set them fluttering. Faith thought fleetingly of Robert, his shining brown eyes and black curly hair, his broad grin, the warmth and strength of his arms and the huskiness of his voice when he had murmured 'Oh, Faith!' into her neck, but she resolutely banished thoughts of him whom she knew she could never have and looked instead at the intense hazel eyes and the regular features of the pleasant face before her and nodded, 'Yes, Stephen, I will.'

~~~

The morning of Faith and Stephen's wedding day dawned bright and breezy. Puffy white clouds scudded across a blue sky sweeping shadows over the hillsides. Bales of straw stood about in fields left yellow with stubble.

Faith was dressed in a simple but charming gown her mother had made for her from a length of cream silk presented to her by Maurice Bosanquet. Her sister, Rebekah, helped her arrange her abundant chestnut hair into an elegant chignon and wove into it some creamy-yellow, sweet-smelling honeysuckle from the hedgerow. She was getting married from North Hill House and, taking care not to snag or dirty her dress, she went to her favourite vantage point for a last look out over the countryside of her birth. The following day she and Stephen were leaving for Bath for him to take up his new teaching appointment.

Faith had mixed feelings about leaving what was familiar. Part of her was sad at saying farewell to her family and this valley she had scarcely ever left. Another part of her could not wait to escape the confines of a small community and see what life was like in the world outside. She might even have the chance to develop her singing – Stephen had mentioned the possibility of lessons – and perform in public. She was excited at the prospect of living in Bath and, at the same time, a trifle apprehensive.

The parish church in Torrington being completely in ruins after the explosion on the night of the battle, Faith and Stephen were to be married in the church at Little Torrington. They would walk to the service with their families. The Roundhead landlord, Richard Stevens, was allowing the married couple to return to North Hill House in his carriage and to use the linhay which fronted onto the courtyard next to the stables for their wedding breakfast. Faith would meet Stephen's parents for the first time and his brother who was to act as best man. Stephen had been unwilling to ask him, at first, his brother being a simple fisherman with no great command of words. He had toyed with the idea of asking if his young master, Miles, would do him the honour of performing the role, but Faith recoiled from this idea and persuaded him that his own family would be more appropriate and that he had no need to feel ashamed of them. Her father would be giving her away and Rebekah and Naomi were to be her bridesmaids.

Faith felt a light tap on her shoulder and turned to find Zillah proffering a posy of wild flowers: reddish-mauve field scabious, white clover with its trefoil leaves and delicate pink herb robert encircled by feathery green ferns. 'For good luck,' said the gypsy woman solemnly.

Faith felt pinned by the flecked gaze. 'Will you come to the church?' she asked.

'I think not, thank 'ee kindly, but I wish you well.' She briefly laid a roughened brown hand on Faith's arm and murmured, 'Be sure,' before turning away and disappearing from view amongst the trees leaving Faith feeling somewhat disconcerted as she looked after her.

Faith placed the pretty little posy in a jar of water in the pantry while she went up to her room and packed the last of her belongings in the small wooden trunk that Stephen had given her. It was not until she was walking up the lane towards Little Torrington with her family, radiant in her lovely dress, the silk smooth and cool against her bare legs, that she remembered it. 'Zillah's flowers!' she exclaimed, stopping in her tracks and turning back. 'I must get them.'

'There isn't time,' Sarah said. 'We can't keep everyone waiting.'

'I must have them!' Faith was surprised at her own vehemence and, before anyone could stop her or offer to go in her place, she started back down to the gateway of North Hill House and along the drive, the gypsy's words, 'be sure', echoing in her mind to the rhythm of her rapid footsteps.

'You'll get all hot and bothered and untidy!' her mother's voice carried down to her but she felt oddly compelled to continued.

Returning with her posy clasped in fingers that were now hot and sticky, something made Faith hesitate in the gateway and look to her left down the road where, earlier, a steady trickle of folk had made their way up towards the church. Even now, there was someone in the distance toiling up the hill: a lone figure leading a horse. Something about that person made Faith's breath catch in her throat.

'Come along, child! We'll be late,' chided her mother from further up the hill where she and her husband, Naomi, Rebekah and Will Avery were waiting for her in the shade of the trees. But Faith stood transfixed watching the man and his horse draw gradually nearer. Suddenly her heart gave a great leap as she realised that the man was walking with a slight limp. Without a second's hesitation, she lifted up her silk skirts and started running down the hill towards him.

The End

BIBLIOGRAPHY

Alexander, J J and Hooper, W R – *The History of Great Torrington in the County of Devon* (Norwich, 1948)
Andriette, Eugene A – *Devon and Exeter in the Civil War* (David & Charles, 1971)
Barfoot, Audrey – *Homes in Britain*
Burrell, Roy – Oxford Junior History 3: *The Tudors and Stuarts* (Oxford University Press, 1980)
Coldharbour Mill leaflet – *The Cottage Industry Spinning and Weaving*
du Maurier, Daphne *The King's General*
Fiennes, Celia – *Through England on a Side Saddle* from *Early Tours in Devon and Cornwall* – a reprint with a new introduction by Alan Gibson of the volume edited by R Pearse Chope first published in 1918 (David & Charles, 1967)
Fraser, Antonia – *The Weaker Vessel* (George Weidenfeld and Nicolson Ltd, 1984)
Gaunt, Peter – *The Cromwellian Gazetteer* (Alan Sutton and The Cromwell Association, 1987)
Gray, Todd – *Devon Household Accounts 1627-1659* (Devon and Cornwall Record Society, 1995)
Hill, Christopher – *The Century of Revolution 1603-1714* (Nelson, 1961)
Hoskins, W G – *A New Survey of England: DEVON* (1954)
Lampard-Vachell, B G – *Wild Birds of Torrington and District* (Geo. Copp, Torrington, 1944)
L'Estrange, Ewen C – *History of Surnames of the British Isles*
Macaulay, Rose – *They Were Defeated* (Collins)
Mann, J de L – *The Cloth Industry in the West of England 1640-1880* (Oxford University Press, 1972)
Scott, A F – *Every One a Witness: The Stuart Age*

Sichel, Marion – *Costume Reference 3: Jacobean, Stuart and Restoration* (B T Batsford Ltd, London)
Sprigg, Joshua – *Anglia Rediviva; England's Recovery* (London M.DC.XLVII) (Oxford University Press)
Steel, Anne – *Living History – The Stuarts*
Sutcliff, Rosemary – *Simon* (Oxford University Press)
Sutcliff, Rosemary – *The Rider of the White Horse* (Hodder & Stoughton)
Young, Peter – *An Illustrated History of The Great Civil War 1642-1648* (Spurbooks Limited)

If you have enjoyed reading this book
and would like to find out
more then read

"THE FORGOTTEN BATTLE"
TORRINGTON 1646
by John Wardman

Available from the
Mole & Haggis Bookshop
Torrington - Tel: **01805 624150**

Published by *Fire & Steel 350 Ltd.* at £15